Judith
Duchesne

Judith Duchesne

A novel by
LYNDA SARGENT

Prepared for publication by
Richard Sargent French

CROWN PUBLISHERS, INC.
NEW YORK

Printed in the United States of America
Published simultaneously in Canada by
General Publishing Company Limited

Library of Congress Cataloging in Publication Data

Sargent, Lynda.
    Judith Duchesne: a novel.

    I. Title.
PZ4.S24828Ju (PS3569.A688) 813'.5'4 79-14294
ISBN 0-517-53905-5

Preface

Lynda Sargent, the author of this novel, is now (April, 1979) eighty-two years old and is confined to a convalescent hospital, a victim of senile dementia. The story is hers, though I have made numerous small changes, principally for the sake of clarity. I have invented no character and no incident; the fiction remains substantially as she herself wrote it.

Lynda worked on this story sporadically for several years. In 1937 she wrote a weekly column for a Carmel, California, newspaper and in it she told an abbreviated, uncopyrighted version of the story. In 1944 she evidently submitted portions of the tale to a literary agent, who reacted effusively and passed the manuscript on to a New York publisher with high hopes. Again, in the early 1950s, a few chapters were read by an executive editor of a major publishing house, and Lynda, according to her letter to one of her sisters (my mother), was encouraged to submit a finished version. She never did. She was "too busy living," she used to say.

Yet the work seems to me to be whole. I hope you will agree.

Carmel Valley, California   RICHARD SARGENT FRENCH

Judith
Duchesne

One

I̲T is the hour when the forepaw of
the day has placed one crimson spoor upon the granite tonsure of the
mountain. The sun, coming up behind the col that divides the breasts of
the Uncanoonucs, far eastward, touches to mottled amber the tips of the
corn shocks that stand in drunken disarray on William Jewell's south
hang and brightens the bellies of the pumpkins that play like children at
hide and seek around their skirts. By the stump fence across the road from
the house, one ancient maple shrieks her bawdy blood-red greeting to the
dawn. And all over the valley of Schoodac Brook the goldenrod gossips
sweetly with the joe-pye weed, and the stretching of bird wings may be
heard.

The mantle of early October is flung over the shoulders of New
Hampshire, and there is no lovelier thing in the world. Yearlong, field
and hill have stood in fealty to the seasons, to grim winter, to reluctant
spring, to the sweats of the workaday summer. Now the duty of earth is
done, seeding to harvest. The apple bough, but lately bowed down with
its bearing, flies up from the burden; the root of the vine rests from the
greed of suckling. It is the menopause and earth in love again. Over her
aging groin the heats of late passion rut, and from woodland to weedlet

bellows the lust of colors, copper and thin gold, all reds, and the tender blaze of the pinks. The weft of the bluejay echoes the blue blue sky. All, all is a singing, and the song is a coronach.

Over the valley of the Brook, old Kearsarge Mountain holds suzerainty. His, the lean leavings of the ice cap, the unyielding ringstreaked gneiss above the peneplain. His, the love of his people. His, the whole benison of the little valley at his feet.

Far up under his indifferent easterly chin an old and solitary pine stands, leaning against the lavender-lichened hip of a boulder, keeping a toehold on life. Its cones drop into Iddo Myrick's chicken run, and on its truncated tip the carrion crows mutter sleepily of the coming day. At its feet the chipmunks, anxious against the winter, scamper and scold, their cheeks like mumps. A trickle of resinous bleeding still drips from an old welt on its shank, where a lightning strike, long long ago, scarred its sapling flesh and ploughed the earth with fire. And out from under its dying master root a bubble of water, like a wee hairless mouse, creeps and creeps.

A rill, where bird beaks cool.

A rivulet to lave the nose hairs of a fawn.

Meandering about Iddo's steep pastureland, mating with secret spring and hidden bog, she succors the high blueberry bush, the bracken and rose-red hardhack, until, by mutual concord with the earth, she has become the Brook.

Some hold that the name given her is of Algonquin origin. But the homefolk along her banks, the people of Schoodac District, will have it otherwise. They tell how, in the early days, when the first sawmill came to plunder the forests of the virgin pine, the saws themselves screeched at the outrage, crying raucously all the day: Schooo...dac, Schooo...dac, Schoo...dac....

In times long gone, when all New Hampshiremen built their stockades on the hillcrests, the better to catch sight of a tomahawk in the valley below, the Brook had been dammed up down at the timberline to make a drinking hole. Here, now, the matted embrace of old water-lily roots moves with the wash of the waters, and in late June their lovely petals open among the pads. Here, too, in the days of Judith Duchesne, the golden trout of New Hampshire came up to spawn.

Now the Brook hurtles down the mountainside, sometimes in waterfalls, hissing under the overhang of maidenhair as if young hamadryads came down to whisper amongst themselves and comb their curls. Sometimes it pauses in purpled pools to rest the lean fingerling fish, or to feel the fur of otter swimming across. Sometimes it lies frowning like a child in sleep, in dreams of the mother sea. And all down its course the huge boulders, old widows of the ice cap, squat on their bare backsides midstream.

Close to the foot of the mountain a gigantic upheaval of rock forms Devil's Cave, once a refuge for runaway slaves; now, in the span of this tale, the place whence may be heard, on a dour wintry evening or under the summer moons, the weird and mournful melody of a giant and his dog, serenading a lady.

Two

N o old-timer of this remote little valley that lies between the Merrimack and the Connecticut, nor the descendants who tell stories around their dinner tables to this day would think to begin the tale of Judith Duchesne without first setting the stage upon which she played out her role. Lovingly they dwell upon the haunting French-heeled footsteps in the great white mansion down by Joppa Bridge, lovingly they call back from the many-memoried past the person of the Countess Kazan de Coqueville, who married the name of Jewell.

Now the Brook has lipped under the overhanging branches of the immense weeping willow tree, which has shed her topaz and verdigris teardrops into the old swimming hole there since she and Sabina were saplings together. Then, muscling around the jutting ledge that marks the boundary of the William Jewell acres, the waters riffle in shallow silence past the James Jewell house, as if atiptoe not to raise its ghosts.

In the first half of the eighteenth century, Jeremiah Jewell the elder, having coughed up his lifeblood with a diphtheria that also took five of Amabel's children, twin sons fell heir to all the Jewell lands. They were of a total dissimilarity. Young Jeremiah, root-bound of New Hampshire, tilled her soil, and his eyes saw the end of the furrow and his hands knew the ox goad. But James was Amabel's son, thrice-blessed, for his was Yankee cunning and the sun dog's halo and out of a blade of grass he made a word and a sword. By the time they had attained their first manhood, they did not speak to each other in the field, though James tried, and more than once they had threatened to reenact the first brother bloodlet.

On the death of their father they halved their inheritance, and James, having heard of the view from Blue Job by the sea, walked thither one morning and went to sea in one of Amabel's brother's clipper ships. Already master of the Greek and Latin languages, in which his mother had schooled him by the light of one candle after the rest of the family was abed, James had it in his mind that he would see every port in the world, would read all the books, and would make his obeisances to the highborn ladies, upon one of whom he would bestow the Jewell name.

A New Hampshire man is as good as his word. By the time James was in his fifties, he had captained his own bottoms to all points of his solid-gold pocket compass, had dined with Voltaire, supped with the great Catherine, translated Epictetus into Sanskrit, and established a countinghouse for thaler and gulden and even the despised pistareen, which multiplied under his gaze. The forty-odd rooms of his mansion outside the city of Portsmouth were furbished in the height of taste with the handicraft of the Near and Far East, and his sense of humor was evidenced in the handpicked black servitors who trod his Persian carpets, for James was of somewhat short stature and none waited upon him who did not stand six feet and five on his bare black soles. These loved him, though they had come princely in his dark holds, for James commanded both love and respect, and in pride and deference they poured his o-be-joyful for his breakfast and at dinnertime served the Madeira that had been twice around the Horn for a good shaking up out of a silver ewer into goblets of chased gold.

But he had not married. He had, indeed, made his obeisances to many highborn women, but for all his wit and wanderings James was not a figure of romance, and he seemed doomed to be liked rather than loved. Withal, he was a novice knight and had much of Amabel in him.

He sat one early evening chatting with Marie Antoinette when Kazan, Countess de Coqueville, came into the room. As was often his wont, he had been absently fingering his pocket compass. He raised his eyes from his *accueil*, glanced at the compass, and found her in line with the polestar. They married within the month and sailed for a shore exceedingly foreign to the Russian widow of a French courtier.

Kazan lacked little in height and nothing in the dark mysteries of her nature in comparison with the blacks who willingly and automatically bent the knee to this imposing mistress. Russian by birth, she had something of the same simple directness and much of the pride of the New Hampshire Jewells. She was ugly to an almost supernal beauty and there was race in every bone of her. Since the day of her unfortunate marriage at the age of fifteen, she had yearned for her homeland with a terrible nostalgia, and when James, speaking to her in the fluence of her native tongue, had told her of New Hampshire Province, of the white birch forests and the snow-bowed branches of the winter fir, of the wolves that howled by Schoodac Brook and the aborigines his grandfather had killed from the cupola of the barn, she was afire like a girl to see this last new land which James vowed was so like her own.

In later years, she told Hester Jewell, Jeremiah's wife, that she had been on the point of taking vows when she met James. That she took James instead was no surprise, for Kazan was no Saint Theresa, and she had a certain curiosity about a naked redskin in war paint who had so very original a manner of dealing with the scalp of an Englishman. That she could sit at dinner in a forty-room house, holding the stem of a golden goblet in her long strong fingers, and listen in complete comfort and safety to wolf cry and war whoop in the virgin forest just outside, was more than Kazan could forbear to try.

She crossed the Atlantic wearing the rubies James had given her for a wedding present, and in the hold were piled the boxes of velvets and China silks, of gauds and furbelows, and all her court finery. In the bodice of her gown she carried a sheaf of legal papers noting the fortune James had bestowed upon her. Among them was the deed to the Schoodac property.

For the first five years of their union, Kazan made a sensation in the great houses of Portsmouth, and she gave James much pleasure, for she had a gift of listening which is the first law of entertainment, and her heart was tender. But it was not a love match. And when, to the surprise of all her friends, she fell in love with the wilderness along the Brook, James built her a house there.

Kazan was in her early forties when she first came to Schoodac to spend the summers. James had done well by the house, for he was fond of his wife even if she never took, in his heart, the room he had there for the sea and the space he saved apart for his books. The mansion was early colonial, spacious and elegant, and the signature of the court of Catherine was inscribed on the crest of its lovely front doorway. Ikon and samovar of workmanship beyond price had been brought from the city on the Baltic. Twelve of the blacks, selected for their unquestioned loyalty to their mistress and for their great strength and cunning, attended Kazan when she was in residence there, and, except for an occasional visit from James, she never invited guests.

It is said that her simplicity of manner, her delight in the countryside, her way with a sick child, and the music of her voice captivated even Jeremiah. For Hester she conceived a deep love, and of a summer afternoon they might be seen, she and Hester, bent over their needlework, whilst pretty young Winsome Jewell, Hester's daughter, did her French lessons, and the enormous white wolflike dog, who looked as if he had been designed for a hearth rug, rested his watching nostrils on the tip of his mistress's slippers. Morning and evening, Kazan walked in her garden while four of the blacks stood watch with swords.

Shorter and shorter grew the Portsmouth season, and Kazan began coming early in spring for the mayflowers and staying until snowfall. Hester wrote in her diary: "It is like, with her, as a second childhood, for she is sooth more girlish than Winsome in her ways. She tells me she has never been happy since her parents married her off at the preposterous age of fifteen, without so much as consulting her wishes in the matter. I declare, it is pleasuresome to be acquainted with so greit a Lady, and such a merrie one."

It was a late October night in the last year of the eighteenth century, and the first snow had fallen. Kazan descended the grand staircase in full court dress, which set her off perfectly, and seated herself by the fire in the drawing room. A profound sadness was over her. She could not bring herself to return to Portsmouth, and when she took her glass of wine from the devoted hands of Old Boo, who had consecrated his life to her service, he read her mind.

"Madam will forgive me for speaking, but it is in my mind that she desires not to leave this house for the winter."

Kazan, Countess de Coqueville, lifted her gloaming eyes to those of the slave.

"Boo, I never know how it is that you read my mind."

"My lady, it is the heart one reads. I have consulted with the servants. We remain with you gladly. I have also talked with Mister Jewell, who will provide us with firewood. Tomorrow, if it be your wish, I will send Neekosh with message to the Master. There is no need for fear. I have learned the language of the sachems, and we have muskets and powder."

"But the Master, Boo. He likes me there for the parties."

"The Master writes his great book this winter. He has been pleased to honor me with this confidence."

"I don't know what I would do without you, Boo. Without your wisdom. Yes, send your messenger."

After Boo had bowed himself out, Kazan sat and sipped her wine, her heart at great ease. James would not greatly miss her; would even, perhaps, be somewhat relieved. That he had not spoken to her about beginning the record of his life and travels, so long projected, could only mean that he did not wish to interfere with her pleasure in the social season of the colony. Now it had come out all right. Her life was at last her own. She could see Winsome through with her preparation for the academy. There was Hester's journal, which she was sure was worthy of publication. There was, indeed, much that she could do here in the wilderness, where the scattered settlers were ever in some sort of need, needs that her purse and her capable hands could assuage. A sigh of pure content passed the still girlishly red lips of the Russian-born lady. After all, there were more ways than one in which to take vows.

Yes, yes, she thought, and heard the front door wrenched open with a thunderous wracking and the unmistakable howl that was a war whoop.

At the door of the drawing room stood a man. He was such a figure as Kazan had once imagined when James first told her of the Pennacook chiefs. From the beaded white headband to the beaded white moccasins, he was dressed in the snowy skins of the winter councils. Kazan's first thought was that she had never seen a handsomer or grander human figure. The musket in his hands was leveled at her eyes.

Without haste, the Lady Kazan rose to her feet, and he was taller than she. She, too, was wearing white, her ivory-white satin, and her rubies and the candlelit Madeira whispered of blood, of lifeblood and death. Her small tiara was aflame with diamond and ruby fire, and the long fingers that held the stem of her wineglass were clusters of twinkling lights, steady.

When she spoke there was no flinch in the throaty beauty of her voice. She lifted her glass.

"Good greetings, friend," she said. "*A votre santé.*"

The musket lowered. The ebony of barbarian eyes looked straight into the matching black of the savage's.

Kazan had a long moment to wonder what had happened to the twelve loaded muskets which she knew protruded invisibly through doorway, from behind tapestry, from the trapdoor in the ceiling above her head. Then Old Boo came silently across the carpet, decanter in hand, and, making his handsomest obeisance, proffered the guest a glass. With a grimace that was half smile, half challenge, and with all the gentle suavity of his race, he took the musket from the redskin's hands.

When Kazan's lover left the house at moondown, near dawn, he placed beside her pillow a perfect strand of wampum, such as only haughty sachems wore. Kazan was never seen in her rubies again.

It is said along the Brook that the paramour of the Lady Kazan was a lineal descendant of the mighty and beloved Passaconaway, come down from Saint Francis in Canada that night in blood vengeance on the Jewells for the slaughter of his people by Jeremiah and Amabel from the cupola of the barn. Seeing the blazingly lighted great house and figures moving about—for Kazan never drew her curtains—he had thought to reap his whole harvest there. The neighbors gave Kazan due credit for saving the lives of all that night, and, being of an expedient ilk, with no Puritans amongst them, profited by the presence of a friendly Indian in their midst, and for the most part desisted from comment on the state of Kazan's affairs.

In an ancient metal box in Mary Trumbull Jewell's bedroom, the original copy of Hester Jewell's diary rests. Here may be read the concluding words of the legend.

There be a greit sorrowe in my heart this night, for I have lost my best frend on this earthe. Little did I think, in this mortal flesh, to know so wondrously fine a ladye. It is not for such a Poor Person as me to Judge of Her connexion with a Man who was not Her Married Husband, but if the Wrath of Almighty God descend upon me for thinking as I do, let him strike me Deade for saying that I have never Known a Truer Marriage of Soules. She Shared her greit Pleasure and Happiness with alle, and the Healing in her Hands was a Gifte from on High, for no Mortal soul in this Settlement went without the Blessing of her Presence, and the Poore who are always with us She Helped beyond the Call of Necessitie. The

Lowliest were Her Frends, and if the Goode book sayeth Truth, that the greitest Virtue is Charitie, she had More Virtue than any Soule I have known in these Seventie and Three years of my Life.

I have been Witness to her going this night. She lay upon her greit bed and a Sweeter sighte I have never seen than the Manner of her Passing. Of late she had grown very Olde, and her Tallness had shrunk so that it Seemed a Little winde would blow her Off. He was there Beside her, holding Her hand. I kneeled at the foote of the bed and Prayed to God that He might not take her, but She Smiled and said it was Time now. When she Breathed her Last, he Picked her up in his Arms, as if she were a Feather, though he, too, is Old, and Carried her away.

I saw Them go. He bore her Bodie towards the North. God Rest Her Beautiful Soule.

Kazan had gone on the Lone Wolf Ride with the last of the mighty sachems ever to be seen in New Hampshire.

Three

LONG before anyone else in the District has kneaded the raising day with wakings, before moondown, before the yawning of crows, old Sabina Dow turns homeward. She has been over Salisbury way this night, heckling the calfmoon with sighs and incantations, in the swamp where Freckle Pond sends its tithe to Schoodac Brook. On the instant of midnight, she has heard the wind come up and in it the keening gad of things to come, the momentous supersonic which is hers for the listening.

No one knows Sabina's exact age, but from old diaries and by whisperings and susurrations handed down, folks reckon she must be well over a hundred. Her puny acre does not touch upon the Brook, but in fee simple of quick dark memory, and long possession of its root and stalk, and by the mystic way of water running, all the reach and fetch of the burn is hers. She lives in her small tumble of a log house, up the road a piece from the William Jewell place, and how she lives but by her wit of earth itself has long since ceased to be a vexation to her neighbors.

Into her basket this morning she has carefully placed a root of sassafras, a fistful of pipsissewa and sweet flag for bitterness and beauty. Under the gathering a frozen froglet lies, stretched out in all his length, dug up from his winter mud, dug with her old bony claws that are strong with the clutch and clamp of many dooms. The urgency that drove her forth on the first surd syllables of the wind still moistens her pewter skin, and her ebony eyes fly and fly, palping with secret wantonness all things they touch, coming back to sit above her nose like wizened buzzard birds, uneasy on a bough.

And as she goes, whithering in the mist like a disembodied spirit moving rootless from hummock to hummock, she trails alongside her the legend of her life.

Legend of her mother, a towering Highlands girl, following her British bridegroom into the wilderness, bringing with her a tall young savage, the first black slave ever known in these parts. Leftenant Fitzwilliam Dow had come to mark the virgin pine for masts in the Royal Navy. After he, with the help of the black, had hewn out the logs for the cabin, and furnished it with a stockade for the protection of his wife, he went on northward under the shadow of the Great Stone Face and was never seen again.

There is no true evidence of the chemic of Sabina's blood, but neither is there any doubt about it. William Jewell, at sixty-five, remembers her in the prime of her life, when the subtle seeping delicacy of her chiaroscuro skin shone in candlelight like still serpents, and her long blue-black hair kinked in the rain. Her eyes, William's father had said, might have been her mother's, for there was much of the dark Scot in her, but for the lure and listen in them. And all her jungle beauty, soft and wild, came to life in her dusky eiderdown voice, speaking the lust of mating butterflies who fold and unfold their wings in opposite directions at once.

William's father, coming home along the darkening trails one night from fishing over Winnepesaukee way, was witness to a sight that haunted his dreams for the remainder of his life. Trudging wearily at the end of his long trek, he saw out of the corner of his eye the glow of fire, and smelt an odious stench. The fire was offside the trail, between the stockade and the Brook, and fearing for his own house, he searched it out. Nearing, he was stopped in his tracks by the sound of voices, of cries unearthly, of a chanting that made his blood run as cold as his own father's had at the sound of a war whoop.

He crept forward on his belly, his loaded musket pointed.

In the middle of a cleared circle of the forest a scene was being enacted which loosened his grip on his gun, and the sweat ran cold along his loins. On top of a pile of resinous pine boughs lay what remained of the head of Sabina's mother, the long black hair curling upward Medusalike, a placid smile on the blood-red face. Around the fire, hand in hand, danced the savage and the small girl, and her soft fresh voice was a reluctant melodious counterpoint to the shriek and wail of the man, so that it could not be told whether she was weeping or rejoicing. In his free hand, the black held a homemade spear, its whetted edge gleaming in the light of the fire as he brandished it, now high, now close to the fire, in the contortions of the dance. Man and child were naked, but, face and body, they were cunningly daubed with all color, and in their ears and on ankle and arm, circlets of brass leapt with their own separate flames.

William Jewell, senior, lay bewitched, his musket forgotten, the stink of human flesh acquainting his nostrils. The fire died a little. The child, lagging with weariness, fell sobbing beside the crackle of the breaking pine branches, and the savage laid down his spear and took her to his naked breast. Then, her small dark arms clutching about his neck, he rocked her tenderly, crooning a jungle lullaby. The throat that had a moment before sent raucous ejection of fiend and barbarian was now the mother voice, the split reed for all tuning.

William Jewell was not an unlearned man. His British forebears had been country squires, bookish men, and William knew something of the ways of the dark continent. It had been rumored that the Scottish woman ailed, and if this was their way with the dead, it was none of his business. He waited while the black said his last muttered invocations over the embers, meanwhile casting handfuls of ashes over the ashes of the woman, and then went off toward the log house with the sleeping child. William got up and went home. The Jewells were close-mouthed folk, and as likely as not no one would ever have known about William's experience had not another witnessed a more ravishing scene.

The Puritans came late to New Hampshire, but by the first quarter of the nineteenth century, two hundred years after the Strawbery Banke settlement, a scattering had dribbled in. One such, on some night errand, came later to the cleared circle in the forest. Sabina was then a girl, perhaps twelve years old, a slender sapling of desire. The settler heard the furious demon cries and bellied toward the fire.

The dance that night was the choreography of lust. Now tossing his spear in deft convolutions high in air, now matching the motion of the weapon with the thrust of his gigantic erect phallus, the savage pursued the girl, leaping with throaty cries upward, forward, crabwise, withdrawing, approaching, catching at hair and nipple and buttock, while Sabina executed her elusive deliberate witchery, her sinuous body lustrous against the flames, her small breasts erect and flaunting, her long black hair curling upward, upward in the flames' draught, upward into the night of magic, upward beyond reach and belief. Rhythms of ancient faiths, fecundity, and supplication, faiths begotten of night and innocent appetency, immingled with the turning wind and the rise and fall of moontides.

The Puritan saw the dance as in a dream, enchanted. He saw the fantasy of embrace, and the reality, his muscles limp, his will and all his

God-fearing gone down to mix with his own desire. This conquered, and in terror of rage and concupiscence, he rose up and leapt out and sank the abandoned spear between the glistening dark shoulder blades.

Sabina threw herself upon the pyre where her father and her lover lay in the common blood. This act brought the settler somewhat to his senses, and he snatched the girl into his arms and dragged her home. His wife, bellied high with child, came out of the sitting room to find, standing erect and fierce in the middle of her kitchen floor, the wanton figure of a wild woman. The two women stared with mutual hatred.

"What sort of creature have you brought into this Christian house?" the wife asked.

But before the man could reply, Sabina lifted her head and heard the wind go by, and in it the lash of the gad. And she herself spoke, in the garbled, only half-intelligible words she had learned from mother and father.

"Ar doom," she said. "Ar coom un daith upon ar wind. I ken...I ken."

It was spoken in a voice that seemed not at all to come from so slight and young a thing, as it had been said through and not by her, as if the pluckings from the breasts of cygnets had fallen across the candlelight.

Folks say, but this may be apocryphal, that the woman dropped dead in her tracks. At any rate, Sabina had eased out into the night, going like a wraith between the ankles of the air.

Sabina knows the burn as no man else. Swamp adder and henbane root, crawling wee beasties of ooze and slime, sough woody branches overhanging the pool, drought of August and dream of April noon, and the fruitful, conjugal, concealing night. The people of Schoodac District do not exactly take Sabina for granted, for she may, at any hour of day or night, appear on a door rock, foretelling doom. No neighbor has ever been inside her house, but Sarah Gooden and Mary Jewell, meeting her on the road or in the meadow, accost her kindly, and she will speak of beauty then, or violence, or any primal innocence, in words they do not quite understand, but the sense of which is always clear.

There is little mysticism in most New Hampshiremen, but no New Hampshire woman lives without it, as she would not live without a kettle for deep-frying her doughnuts; and the legend transmutes into the myth. The neighbors do not heed Sabina now, from one day to the other, until they hear her voice, rising with the wind.

Four

O<small>N</small> its way down to the Trumbull meadow, the Brook thrusts an impertinent elbow into a corner of the Goss farm.

Bertie is standing sucking his tongue, a habit he has never quite got over. He has just taken the milk pails from their pegs at the back kitchen door, where they have been trying to warm their bottoms in the first dubious heat of the day. He is thinking of his mother, that it is she jangling pots and iron spiders in the house. No, no. It's only Saphronia Goss, his wife. Funny that he has a wife. He's never got over that, either.

One by one, he plucks grapes from the old Concord arbor over the back porch, plopping them into his suckling mouth. His mouth is an orifice from which the eye turns away. Bertie doesn't seem so very different from the small boy who used to ride horsey on the old stump down by the woodshed, partly because it made his fat mother jealous, partly for other reasons. It is really hard to say whether Bertie has any face at all, so indifferently got up it is, an afterthought face. Like some women, it's Bertie's backsides that give him his character. A fine pair of bosoms, with his overalls stretched tight across them, and the crack showing plain. They move when he moves, when he waddles about on those feet that were made for ballet slippers. Strong men, walking down the road behind him, think with secret shame of putting their hands there.

The Goss farm is one of the most prosperous in the District and one of the prettiest. Its fertile uplands, lying along the old Kearsarge Gore, burgeon with the heavy beards of wheat, and Bertie's Guernseys and Rhode Island Reds share honors with William Jewell's at the county fairs. For the love of the earth that gives of its hot milks, of the fat udders of his cattle, of the sleek feathering of all fowls, is all of Bertie's love. When he plucks and pinfeathers a warm hen, he puts it against his cheek if Phronie isn't watching, and smiles, and his face comes to life.

I oughtta take that stump out, he thinks for the thousandth time. It's a perfect target for a lightning strike. But he can't do it. Something about the hard upthrust, the untiring erection, forbids.

From the kitchen comes the ratchet of Phronie's voice, whetting on the abrasive of her tongue, calling to him to get his chores over with. He has been thinking of his mother again, of her warm flesh, her great udders.

"Aw, it's only Phronie, a-running off at the vowels," he says under his breath, using a phrase he coined about her fourteen years ago, just after their marriage. There is a little cruelty in his eyes and hands as he clutches back at the handles of the day again.

Saphronia Tewksbury Goss trots from buttery to bake oven to breakfast table, crop forward like a running pullet. Her lean fingers tap the golding crust of her saleratus biscuits with light quick passion.

About Phronie there is not a single recognizable item left of the young Tewksbury girl who married Bertie Goss. She was nineteen then, and nubile with the freshness of an opening cowslip bud, all gold and dewstruck, blinking her golden eyes at any sun. Picked bone she is now, bone in a dry valley, all sinew, muscle of strong heart, tendon of shank and loin, a hard fibre all of one piece. The echo of old bitterness runs in her tongue, and some who call her a gossip, some of the women, will add that they'd just as soon not be married to Bertie, not that Bertie isn't a good man, but . . .

Her secret she carries like a white stone under her busy tongue, like something she must not swallow lest it enter into her. Phronie's got a good heart, is what they say about her, when she leans forward over her knitting to speculate over the significance of the underwear seen on someone's clothesline.

The biscuits are done, a perfection, as her whole house is a perfection, never permitting herself an idle moment for the evil of desire. She stands by the window, poking her hard fingers around the geraniums, waiting for Bertie to come in. The excitation of the morning, of waking up with Bertie's plump body close to hers, is wearing off, and the shadow of the virginity she has never lost dies from her petrified amber eyes.

"Onward, Christian soldiers," she supplicates, marching with her banner across the big kitchen to hang a fresh roller towel for Bertie's washing-up.

But a niggardly nip the waters take at the Josiah Peavy place, and of that earth there is little goodliness. In his thin wedge of meadow only the matted roots of the sweet flag, the tall spears of cat-o'-nine-tails, and a little mowing of coarsest meadow grass are found. And over all his land, each spring brings a new crop of rocks where there is plowing to be done, and Siah curses God.

Six prime Jersey cows, bony and full of cream as their master, hear the dolorous singsong of Siah's voice . . . coboss . . . coboss . . . , and stir in their stanchions. Siah is chanting the canticle of his beloved: My beloved hath a vineyard on a very fruitful hill. He runnels with slaked and unslaked rapacities, and sees in the slope of his unfruitful upland pasture the holy limning of breast and idol thigh, fingered in beauty by the uprisen sun.

For there is the beauty, the beauty!

It is told of Josiah Peavy that when he was a young man, working in

a glove factory down near Boston, he was quite a blade. A lady's man;
even, they whisper, a drinking man. A smart boy, smarter than most,
with something about him no one in the District understood. As a child,
he would stand up on the old stump fence across the road from the house
and recite poetry or play parson. He worked in the factory to save money
to go to Harvard, but old man Peavy didn't hold with edication, and
Josiah himself never managed to save a penny in his life. When he sells
cream for a living, the top of it is for Sarah. If he timbers off a section,
there is a purebred mare for Sarah's birthday.

He is thinking this morning, as he strips the full udders, that he
would like to be elected to the board of selectmen, come Town Meeting.
But he knows he won't. He isn't popular. He scorns to be popular, but
he'd like to be, all the same. Ozias Fellows will get it. He's slick with
his tongue. He doesn't come right out and say what he thinks. Josiah
wants that new school built. Oh, Ozias is all right, in his skim-milk
way.

Suddenly Josiah feels all the richness again. It rises up in him like a
great tower, for the beauty.

But when he goes to feed the horses, he finds that the off mare has
cast a shoe, and he had meant to haul manure today for the south hang.

"Goddamn my accursed luck," he says.

Up on the old Sawyer place, across the Brook from William Jewell's, a
small dubious man, old before his time, sets a match to a kerosene lamp,
and lays a fire in the stove. He and his boy have just moved in, and there
is a good deal of orderly clutter about, but Fred Cheney is a clean neat
man and he brushes the chips from the stove with a new turkey wing.
Nothing about this man has ever counted for much, and what gumption
he had had was lost with the death of his wife, when the boy was born.
His eyes water with unshed tears, and his hands wander away from him
on errands of no consequence, returning to stir up yesterday's oatmeal,
going back to fetch at their forever unfinished business.

The old torment of irresolution bedevils him this morning, running
amok in his castrated will. Shall he waken the boy, and let him go? Ah,

no. He is safer here. But yes. He likes school, he gets along fair to middling, and don't hurt no one. And he'll never stay long in one place anyway. He might as well be where someone can keep an eye on him, if there be anyone who can rightly keep an eye on him. But what will the kids do to him but make fun of him, and he grinning, grinning at their insults. Well, if he don't like the teacher, he'll be back soon enough, off wandering again.

The boy is sleeping crosswise of the bed his father had already lengthened out for him. One huge bare foot dangles on the floor. Good Lord, Fred thinks, he musta growed a good eighteen inches since spring. The boy grins in his sleep, and his father's heart, already pulped with continuous breaking, crumples within. His love for the boy, and his fear, are like the measureless tumult of an horizonless sea, git and whoa, and no sight of land.

Fred clears his throat.

"Boy," he whispers. "Ed, boy, Time to wake up. School today."

Five

CHRISTOPHER JEWELL, great-grandson of Jeremiah, James's twin, swinging his five-quart lard pail with its cold baked-bean sandwich and pickles and apple pie and slab of cheese for dinner, stivvered in high elation off across the bridge and up the hill that led to the District's hall of learning. A lonely lad, little given to intimacy with other boys, his heart was high with the almost unrecognized hope that he might find, in some new scholar from the other side of the District beyond the bridge, a companion to share the secrets of his life. Like all solitary youngsters, all sensitive, set-apart people, he yearned for that one soul, that co-walker with himself, who would know without speaking, do without asking, give even as he was given to. Such a one he had never found, and, lacking, he countered the distrust of his fellows with a pair of hard competent fists and a contempt he could ill conceal. His was the profound intimacy with earth, the single ruby feather in his pants pocket, the robin eggs safe in the nest, the serpent unhindered on the rock. And if he went out gunning at dawn for the twenty cents' bounty on the head of a crow, he had never descended to a slingshot; he could put a worm expertly on a hook, but he never stepped his foot upon one.

The Schoodac District schoolhouse sat squat against a wooded hill, smug and weatherworn on its granite ledge. In springtime the wild strawberries ruddled its yard and the mouths of its scholars, and June brought a carpet of low blueberries along the stone wall across the road. With the October winds, the chestnuts tossed their burrs on the ground and the red squirrels chattered during lesson hours.

Chris, his pockets stuffed with chestnuts, scuffed up dead leaves, a mite apart from the rest of the scholars, waiting for the teacher to arrive. Quint Haley, from off over Joppa way, mimicked his shuffling. Already, Quint was spoiling for a fight. Chris feigned not to see. He would fight if he had to. Quint was a head taller, but Chris knew every soft spot in him, brain and brawn. They had fought before, but the score had never been settled. Chris knew it could never be settled, but that, too, was his secret. It was Quint's last term in school, and he had two ambitions in life: to sing in the church choir and to rub Christopher Jewell's nose in the dirt.

When the teacher drove up in her buggy Quint swaggered up to unhitch her horse and lead him out into the swamp to graze. Chris, shy and disdaining to be teacher's pet, took a step toward the schoolhouse, and stopped, his eyes riveted on a figure loping up the hill. He had never seen the man before. He had never set eyes on so big a man, though his own father stood six foot four in his socks.

Chris gawked. The stranger plodded into the yard and came to a halt. This was no grown man, but a boy, a new scholar. Sheer incredulity blotted out the morning. The unbelievable apparition came to a halt, grinning down on his mates, his huge face all askew with friendliness. A ridiculously small paper sack of lunch dangled from one enormous hand. The sleeves of his frayed coat came to his elbows, and his pants stopped short above his ankles, leaving his gigantic bare feet, like a pair of drag sleds, way out in front. He must have measured surely seven feet, and all this length was topped by a flying thatch the color of dry cornstalks that shot like restive flames up into the blue, making him look as if the whole ponderous hulk of him might at any moment be borne lightly up and out of sight.

Chris drew one long deep breath of joy. He saw Quint Haley's face cloud down, and heard the muttered oath hang like a wisp of dirty rag, midair.

In the dead silence, Chris stepped forward and returned the smile.

"Hi, you," he said, his voice gone soft with unutterable pleasure, "What's yer name?"

"My paw, he talls me, Bid Ed."

Someone tittered.

"How old be you?" Chris glared at the titterer.

"I be sixteen, tome Tristmas."

"Where'n tunket do you live?"

"I dess they tall it the Ol' Sawyer place."

"Well, by cracky, the Old Sawyer place is right across the Brook from ours. I ain't never seen you before."

"We jest tome, yestidy."

"Huh! How's about some nuts?"

That was the strangest term ever held at Schoodac District School. The teacher, young and inexperienced, was the first woman ever to try to cope with the scholars there. The District extended beyond the bridge to the verge of the village, and the boys who lived beyond the Brook were a tough lot. School kept only for two short terms, and the scholars were often in their late teens before they fulfilled the requirements for graduation. The boys, hardened by labor in field and woodlot, had little interest in fractions and composition, but an infinite capacity to torment the helpless, especially in the female form.

Miss Flanders took one smiling glance at her brood, trying to hide her apprehension. When she saw Big Ed, her face opened with astonishment and it was plain she was afraid.

But she had no need, for, from the beginning, Ed was her slave. She carried, this morning, a heavy load of books, and Big Ed, stepping hurriedly forward, gently took them from her.

"Please, ma'am, tan't I he'p you?" he said, and smiled at her.

The scholars didn't wait for the bell to be rung, but trooped in to see what was going on. It was clear that Big Ed wouldn't fit into any of the seats, and Miss Flanders looked helplessly about. But her fantastic pupil settled the matter himself. He put his lunch down on the bench at the back of the room, the one reserved for visiting parents and school officials, lifted a heavy loose desk from its corner as if it were a basket of feathers, put it tenderly down, and straddled his long legs around it. Then, as much as to say he was ready to do anything else required of him, he grinned at Miss Flanders with such doglike eagerness to please that he seemed to wag all over.

Ed wasn't what you'd call a bright scholar, but he wasn't exactly dumb, either. He could read well enough by the standards of the school, though his spelling was erratic. Geography he loved. He had a passion for the things that grew in strange lands, and you'd have thought he kept a Bengal tiger and a boa constrictor and a mongoose for pets, the way he knew their habits. Once he tried to hop down the aisle like a kangaroo, he was so delighted with the creature. But arithmetic he didn't cotton to at all. With much counting on his fingers, he could add up simple figures, but a problem in fractions was so much Greek to him.

"Ed," Miss Flanders said to him one day, after she had patiently juggled two apples, trying to make him understand one half of two, "what is a fraction?"

Big Ed looked as if he was going to cry. "I . . . I dunno, Miz Flanders. I wish I did."

And that was as far as he ever got in the science of numbers.

It was in singing class that Ed took his honors. There wasn't anything he couldn't do with his voice. If he chose to take the lower parts, out of the very depths of his being came a thunderous bass, as true as a tuning fork, as deep as if it had started down in his mighty toes and gathered tone all the way up. And no little girl in school could match his soprano for its high clear sweetness. Sometimes, with his eyes closed and his big body swaying, he would go right on singing after the others had stopped, the top notes of his improvised melody floating, soft and disembodied, out into the October haze.

But for all Ed's willingness and docility, the term was a bad one for Miss Flanders. The big boys, led by Quint Haley, were bent on mischief anyhow, and when they found that their tricks and schemings fell on the fallow earth of Ed's incomprehension, they took out all their resentment on their poor teacher. Quint had the build and the cussedness of a young bull just feeling his oats, and he had never let a boy his age go unchallenged before. But after a few casual exhibitions of Big Ed's strength, he didn't dare take him on in single combat, and he was vexed almost out of his wits. He wasn't a bully, and, likely as not, if Ed had shown any disposition to settle the matter, he'd have been content to give him his due and enlist his incredible strength on the side of lawlessness and disorder. But Ed accepted their meanest jokes as offices of friendship, and he would just grin at them for outwitting him. He spent most of his recess and noontimes foraging out in the woods by himself, bringing back to Miss Flanders the prizes that were, for one reason or another, out of the reach of the others: a hanging oriole nest, the best apples from the top branches of the Northern Spy over the wall, a neat little chipmunk he had tamed.

Upon finding a large black snake in his desk one morning, he picked it up lovingly and put it down his shirtfront. The school was completely unmanageable that morning, thinking of that snake lying there on his belly, but Ed went right on with his lessons. At recess time he took it out, letting it coil around his arm, and loped off to the edge of the woods, where he put it gently on the ground.

But not before Quint had got it by the tail.

"Goddamn you, you big sissy," Quint yelled. "I'll show you what to do with yer dodratted ol' snake."

He held it high over his head, ready to snap its neck broke. Ed reached for his hand and forced the knuckles open. The snake poured itself into the sweet fern. Quint backed away and squared off, his fists like rocks, but Ed was already out of reach in the woods, Chris Jewell by his side.

Added to his other offenses, Big Ed managed to deprive the rest of the scholars of their time-honored prerogatives. To keep the water bucket filled from the spring outside, to fill the woodbox, to hitch and unhitch the teacher's horse, were privileges customarily meted out equally amongst them. Just how Ed came to be always on hand first to do these things was something of a mystery. Even Miss Flanders's most urgent remonstrances had no effect on him, and he went right ahead as if taking his orders from a higher authority than any there. If he was trying to make up in some way for his difference from the rest, he only succeeded in making it stick out like a boil on the end of your nose.

It was during that first month of school that Chris Jewell was wakened one night by a strange sound. He lay, still half asleep, wondering what in thunderation it could be. It was certainly no noise he had ever heard before, though there was something vaguely familiar about it; a spooky thing, half howling, half singing. Sort of like the sound in the tales Uncle Bart had brought back from the West, tales of coyotes that wailed in the night with an almost human lament, and came down to kill the newborn calf and raid the chicken coop. Chris pinched himself. It might be that he was still snoozing. But, no, he was awake, all right, and there were no such varmints in New Hampshire to howl in the night and come marauding.

The racket wasn't very far away; just across the Brook, Chris figured. Then he remembered the stories that had been going around of a great black dog that had been seen in the countryside. Jake Cogswell, who certainly was no coward, had been coming home from the village one night a while back, and the crittur had leapt across the road just in front of him. It had the shape of a dog and it growled like a dog, but it was bigger than any dog he'd ever seen, and it had scared the spit out of Jake. And Saphronie Goss, whose word was as good as the first chapter of Genesis, had run screaming into the kitchen one evening, blubbering about a bear eating out of the swill pail, though it had been forty years since a bear had been seen in those parts.

By gorry, Chris thought, that's a funny noise for a dog to make. He pulled on his britches and stole downstairs after the shotgun. He wasn't afraid. Nothing on God's green earth could frighten Chris, not so's you'd know it.

Outside in the darkness, he stopped to get his night eyes and take his bearings. Yep, right over in the Sawyer field. He crept down back of the well house and out onto the ledge that jutted into the Brook. It was a lightish night, and he could see quite clearly. "As plain as day," he would say later.

The outcropping of rock that was known as Devil's Cave ran down to the edge of the Brook, and on the topmost boulder sat Big Ed. One arm was thrown around the neck of that all-fired great dog, and they were whooping it up in the weirdest duet ever heard by mortal ears. Chris didn't dare move. There was something about that infernal noise that got you in the pit of the stomach. One moment it would rise to an earsplitting howl, and the next it was just the wafting of a little tune, so soft and sweet you wanted to bawl. Everything else, the night owls and the katydids, had stopped to listen. Chris, who was never in his life able to carry a tune, knew there wasn't a false note in it.

Presently, they got down from the rock pile and meandered off up the hill, Big Ed muttering, "Tome, Dod. Tome on home, Dod."

It took a long time for Chris to get back to sleep. He was terribly excited. He couldn't have said why.

From that time on, Big Ed was something of a hero in Chris's eyes. He dogged his footsteps, keeping at a little distance, for Ed paid scant attention to him. The singing could be heard night after night, but often way off over Kearsarge way, and though the farmers threatened to go gunning for it, so far Chris was evidently sole possessor of its secret, and it tickled him to keep it that way. He kept a weather eye on the boys at school, his hard grimy little fists clenched in his pockets, ready to defend his friend.

He had a couple of fights with Quint Haley. Miss Flanders's horse, a dowdy old mare Chris's father let her use, got mired down in the swamp one morning while Ed was off in the woods, and she refused to budge. The boys yanked at her halter and kicked her in the backsides, but she had got frightened and only thrashed about. Ed heard her whickering and came down to see what was going on. He reached one arm under her belly, spoke a few soft monosyllables, and hoisted her clean out onto solid ground. Quint was mad enough to chew nails. He had to slug somebody, and Chris happened to be within reach. Chris got pretty well mauled up, but he got some satisfaction out of it, too. He knew for whom it was he fought, and he would gladly do it again.

A few days later, on a hot Indian summer morning, a terrible odor spread slowly through the suffocating air of the schoolroom. Finally, Miss Flanders had to ask who, or what, it was that smelled so. Ed looked as puzzled as the rest of them for a minute, then he giggled innocently and pulled from his pocket an old rotten bone. It had been chewed and mouthed, and a few maggots crawled on it.

"School is dismissed for recess," Miss Flanders managed to say, before making a run for the privy.

Ed disappeared into the woods with the bone. When Quint made as to follow, Chris picked a fight with him. It made him feel good and strong, to think of the dog lying out there all the time, waiting, and he fought a kind of delaying action with such fury that he bloodied Quint's nose before he went down under the greatly superior strength of his opponent.

There is nothing like a mystery to get a boy's dander up, and Quint was like a boil ready to bust anyhow. The whole thing came to head a week later. Ed had come to school with an enormous ham bone protruding from his pocket. He left it in the cloakroom with his lunch. Quint excused himself to go to the privy, and when Ed went to look at recess, the bone was gone.

For once, Ed was almost mad. "Who's dot my bone?" he asked with a plaintive sort of anger, the remains of a grin still on his face.

"*I've* dot your consarned ol' bone, te-e-e-cher's pet," taunted Quint. "Why'n't you tome and det it?"

Ed started forward. Just as he did, Chris saw Quint drop the bone and pick up a rock. Then he saw that all the boys had stones. They grouped themselves in a tight phalanx, their faces narrow and intense, their bare feet shuffling eagerly in the dry leaves.

Chris closed in beside Ed. They made a comical picture, big and little, facing the solid sullen front of their adversaries. Quint hauled off and threw his stone, striking Ed on the ear. Then the fracas burst loose. With the stones, they let go all their pent-up savagery, spitting out words they'd never dared to say out loud before, hurling and screeching and slobbering with joy. No longer children, they battled, as all men battle, against the unknown and the feared.

Miss Flanders stood screaming in the doorway, ringing the school bell with furious helplessness.

Big Ed didn't move from his tracks. The grin that had lingered for a moment on his face had turned to piteous disbelief. A trickle of blood ran down from his ear.

As Chris reached blindly for a rock, another one hit Big Ed, this one square on the tip of his nose. He let out a yell of pain. There was a sudden tearing of the bushes, a blood-curdling snarl, and over the underbrush bounded The Dog.

Ed caught him by the scruff of the neck and held him.

"Now, Dod," he said gently. "Now, Dod."

And cupping one hand under his bleeding nose, and paying no attention to the horrified faces of his schoolmates, he went off down the road without a backward look, muttering as he went: "Tome, Dod. Tome on, Dod."

He was never seen at Schoodac District schoolhouse again.

Six

THE white beast, winter, came. In the shrieking of the wind that harried the leaves on the day Big Ed left school forever, the first echoes of its raucous voice were heard. The cattle, browsing, lifted their noses to the north and huddled under the nearest copse for shelter. The silver birch that stood against the wall between the William Jewell place and the big house next door turned her plaintive little palms upward and shuddered. Glistening icicles, like needles from the sewing basket of the rainbow goddess, hung from every rock and root along the Brook. Snow came early that year, and life on the farms folded in upon itself, in house and barn. By Thanksgiving Day the roads were blocked with drifts, and school had shut down for the long winter holiday. Christopher, having passed his entrance examinations to High School, was free from lessons until another October.

Big Ed disappeared after the incident at the schoolhouse, and Chris, busy from daylight to dark with the many tasks his father set him, fretted the days away in lonely apprehension. His conscience vexed him with the thought that he had somehow failed his friend, that he should have beaten Quint to a pulp to show his loyalty. Ed would not fight his own battles, Chris seemed to understand that, judging his friend too square a man to take advantage of his terrible strength. Then, remembering The Dog, he was nagged with a little jealousy, fearful lest the brief felicity of their comradeship was over, and the beast had taken his place. And when the fierce winds blew, he wondered if Ed had shoes—for Chris had never seen Ed's feet enclosed in anything—and if he had a warm jacket and a muffler and mittens against the weather. Snuggled down in his feather bed at night, Chris fell into the first uneasy dreams of his life, alert even in sleep for the raising of the song.

"Christamighty, boy," Uncle Bart said one morning when Chris had haltingly expressed his anxiety to this sympathetic listener, "the boy's a man now. Like as not he's off tomcattin', same's all the rest on us do, come time the old goddamn gits aholt on us. 'Twon't be long before you're at it yerself, my full young sawbuck. Jesus God, it's me that oughter know. Hah! Don't ye tell yer Ma I said so, now."

Chris thought this over, moiling in his mind Big Ed's devotion to Miss Flanders. He didn't believe it was so, somehow, but it troubled him nonetheless.

When Mary Jewell sent him up to bid Fred Cheney to Thanksgiving dinner with them, he found the old man in his neat house, puttering about with many preparations.

"You tell yer Ma, Chris boy, that I sure do appreciate her neighborin'. But I reckon the boy will be back for dinner that day, an' I'm getting things ready. He don't like to eat his grub away from home, ye know. You've missed him, eh? Waal, he comes home most every night, for a spell. Brings that all-fired great hound with him. Makes a devil of a mess, too, lettin' him sleep on his bed thataway. Ayah, that boy's a vexation ter me, an' no doubt."

"Seems he'd be mighty cold."

"Got the hide of an ox, that youngun. Don't seem to feel the cold. I fixed him up with a pair o' rawhide boots. Had that ol' feller down to The Corners, next to Clessie's store, make some to fit. The boy wouldn't have nothin' to do with it, so I had ter measure his feet with a piece of string whilst he was sleepin'. Proud o' them boots! My goodness, he wears 'em to bed, by God."

Mary Jewell was scarcely less concerned about Ed than Chris was, and she sought to comfort her son. "You just be patient, Christopher. Ed's a mooncalf, you know. He's always away at the dark of the moon. Likely as not he's out hunting for it. We must be patient with our friends, to let them go their own way sometimes. You'll see. On the first real moonlit night you may go hunting for him, if he isn't back by then."

And to be sure, on a night when the dichotomous moon fattened in a sky strewn with drifting bright clouds, Chris heard the song again. He had been out to the barn, just before going to bed, to see that a newborn calf was snug, and was running back to the house when the familiar wailing sounded somewhere over Kearsarge way. His mother had heard it, too, and by the time Chris got into the kitchen, she had buttered a fresh loaf, put his muffler on the back of the stove to warm, and was cutting the meat from a hambone.

"Put your rubbers on, and don't wake your father when you go."

Swinging his lantern, Christopher was off. He ran steadily, eagerly, like a young cockerel after a pullet. There was a choking hunk of terror in his throat, for he had never been close to The Dog, except that once. And there was the pervading fear that he might not be wanted any-more. He ran in the direction of the song, and slowed down only when he saw their silhouette atop a knoll under the dark tower of the mountain. Now, like a girl in pursuit of her lover, he wanted to turn back. He wanted Ed to come to him. A great shyness came over him. He remembered what Uncle Bart had said, and felt he was of no consequence to a grown man. He remembered what Mr. Cheney had said about leaving Ed alone. In the paralysis of his emotions, the lantern slipped from his hand and clattered on a rock.

The Dog's plaining changed abruptly to a snarl.

"Why, Dod," Big Ed shouted with peculiar glee, "it's the Boy, it's Tris. Tome on up, Boy. Tome on up here with me an' the Dod. Where've you bin, Boy?"

Chris held out the bone, but The Dog made no move.

"Tome on, Dod. You kin have it. It's a dreat bid bone fer you."

Hardly unbending his haughty neck, The Dog reached and took the bone daintily in his huge jaws, and dropped it between his paws. Chris clambered up beside him, careful not to crowd close. The Dog paid him no attention. The Dog—as he was always known—was never to grant that regal favor to but one other human being besides his master. He would never obey a command, wag his tail, or acquiesce in a caress for any but these two. Where he had come from no one ever learned. He was accepted along the Brook, as Big Ed himself was accepted, as a child of nature in the midst of men, given by the Almighty God for a sign unto his people, to protect, befriend and defend.

Chris was content with this, as with everything that pertained to his friend. He hugged his knees with the joy of reunion, and the thin whey of moonlight dripped from the clabbered sky.

Seven

THE hard winter bellowed up into December with little untoward event. Beautiful . . . ah, beautiful, sleek and innocent-looking, the white beast lay across the land at dawn. Icicles gemmed homely barn and humble house and dripped at noon on frigid nose and ear. The great elm at the James Jewell place wore Kazan de Coqueville's discarded rubies on every twig when the indifferent sun, looking the other way, hurried the brief sky, and the bare trees laid upon the meadows of the snow their grape-wine gossamer of shade. Daylong, betimes, the mute flakes fell, shutting the world beyond the windowpanes behind a dotted dimity veil, and William Jewell dozed after dinner, his stockinged feet on the back of the stove, his pipe bowl resting on his beard. Mary Jewell and Phronie Goss and Sarah Peavy, hanging wash on their lines with the mercury at twenty below, ran back into their houses to warm their bitter-cold hands at their stoves, and saw their clean clothes turn to frozen boards, to flat effigies in flannel petticoat and long red underdrawers.

One late afternoon shortly before Christmas, Mary Jewell, watering the geraniums in her east kitchen windows while waiting for the menfolks to come in to supper, heard sleigh bells, and saw Willie Pike's livery stable rig fighting the drifts up the road.

"Hey, Miz Jewell," Willie yelled as he drove in the yard, "brung ye comp'ny."

A faintness of joy overcame Mary Jewell, rooting her to her tracks. She saw the tall young man disentangle himself from the buffalo robe and heard him fling open the door. Infolded by his arms, she could only sob his name. "John . . . John . . . John . . ."

"There . . . there. Mary . . . little Mary." He put her at arm's length. "How handsome you have grown!"

"And how thin . . . and . . . and worn you are, brother, *dear* brother. And how glad . . . oh, John . . . how glad I am to see you at last. I thought . . . I began to think . . ."

"This is no time for thinking, Mary. Come, quickly, a cup of that strong tea. I must wash out some of Willie Pike's words. Besides, I hear Will coming, and I smell something burning. I could forgive you any deadly sin this minute, Mary, except burning that johnnycake. Oh, johnnycake and milk . . . johnnycake and milk . . . oh!" And he uttered a high wild laugh, so that Mary Jewell, taking the johnnycake out of the oven, thought he had gone mad, and felt nothing but relief from the thought.

"There's enough to talk about, God knows. But it can wait until later . . . after supper. Hello, Will, hello!"

William Jewell gave his hand to his brother-in-law with more than his wonted heartiness. For his wife's brilliant unhappy brother, he had nothing but ungrudging admiration and a profound sense of common suffering, suffering unlike in kind, but shared in understanding. John Trumbull never put on airs about his education. He had the gift of speaking with such clarity of meaning that the words he used, often words William Jewell had never heard, seemed simply to fuse his ideas into a compact whole, as complete as a ripe pear and as easy on the digestion. On his brief visits to the farm he was an able and willing worker, sensing the meaning of a task so that the action required to perform it came about with a nicety of effortlessness which made sweat and sore muscles a part of the joy of doing. William Jewell was a man who never forgot, and he had never forgotten something John Trumbull had done during an earlier visit to Schoodac.

It was after the funeral, and most of the womenfolk had come back to the house to look after Mary. Alone of her four, Christopher had escaped the dread scarlet fever as it ran its course in the countryside. Mary's were the last of the children in the District to be taken, and the weather had turned cold and clear after the early spasm of slashing horror that had brought in the epidemic. Mary, prostrated in body by long nights of nursing, numb in spirit from the still-felt clutch of the greedy hand of death, so much greedier for her than for any other woman around, had been put to bed, and the kitchen was full of womenfolks. Sarah Peavy was weeping soft unclean tears of self-pity for the miscarriage she had had a month before. "Poor . . . poor little mites," she kept sobbing. "Wee posies in God's garden . . ." Phronie Goss countered this with more than usual asperity, having served her tea well from the jug of rum. "Sary, you shut up yer whimperin'. It be the will o' God . . . amen . . . amen . . . amen."

William Jewell, standing with his hands behind his back, warming himself at the stove, was a pillar of stone. John came from his sister's room.

"Come on, Will. She's fast asleep. No need for us here. The barn . . . the barn . . . that's the place for us."

They sat in the old barn chairs, within the warmth of indifferent beasts, the smell of ammonia, of hay, and cow manure.

After a time, John said casually, "We never need to listen, Will, to things we cannot really hear. Women talk. It's their way. Sometimes it seems that all their emotions are in their tongues. That isn't true, but we men have another way. Right now you want to fight, as any man in his senses wants to fight. Well, you can knock me down if you want, though that would be little satisfaction. I'm not God, and you want to take a punch at God. You know something, Will? When we were little tykes, we bawled for our food; we bawled when we were uncomfortable; we bawled for pain, or just being mad at something. Then we were told to be little men, and we never bawled again. When we felt like it, we thrashed some other boy. Christ in heaven, Will, something terrible has happened to you. You have lost your only son, the only one your heart was given to. There you sit, like a stone, asking why? why? why?

Knowing you'll never get an answer, knowing that what's happened to you you didn't in any sense deserve. This isn't a punishment, Will. This isn't something you 'will one day understand,' as that pious old parson blabbered about. This is terror. It is the greatest sorrow of your life. It is too awful for God to have had anything to do with. Cry, man . . . weep all your tears . . . set fire to the barn . . . stop trying to be a little man and be a big one, be a father sorrowing for his child. Come, be a man, Will.''

There was the sound of sobbing in the barn, for John had his own disasters to weep over. A cow lowed, and a burst of agony came up from William Jewell's throat. It towered like a sudden column of forest fire that had been smouldering from a lightning strike. The spiders on the rafters felt it. The horses neighed, and the cattle, forming their mouths into hollow tubes, bawled in concert.

John had slipped from the barn, softly closing its doors. He had stayed another week, silently helping with the chores, quietly doing the right thing at the right time. Most of the week he and Will had spent in the woods, logging. He had never spoken of the incident again. Careful lest he had earned only the resentment of this hard man, he had wielded ax and peavy to the utmost of his strength. But no word of any sort had come from Will. He went without sugar for his tea unless someone passed it to him. The morning John left, he drove him down to the depot at The Corners. When John got down from the sleigh, William held out his hand.

"Come anytime, John. Reckon you'd be mighty handy long about haying time. Bein' ye feel like bringin' yer . . . yer wife an' child here, they be welcome.''

Suppertime was a rejoicing.

"Gosh all hemlock, John. It don't seem this be much on a feast for a prodigal.''

"No one ever seems to realize, Will, that the prodigal was fat and well fed when he came home. If my memory serves me, he had been feasted enough. What he needed was home.''

Mary, watching her brother with love, sensed something exaggerated in his speech, his laughter. She wondered if perhaps sanity had not been kind to him, and withdrawn her harsh cloak, abandoning him to the more clement weather of a little madness. It was clear, though, that her husband was oblivious to anything out of the way, that he was indeed more pleased than she had seen him in many a day.

Later, in the sitting room, the shadows curled with the fireplace flames. Mary sat darning socks, the anxiety in her eyes as deft as the needle in the wool. Chris had been sent to bed, and Bart, sensing a family conclave, had harrumphed an apology and gone to his room.

"No reason for your leaving us, Will," John said, settling into the gooseneck rocker by the fireplace. "Fact, there's something I'd rather like to talk to you about. And you might as well hear what I have to say to Mary. Here, try some of this tobacco in your pipe. A friend sent it from London. A pleasing blend, though perhaps a little mild for your taste." He paused a moment. "Father died last night, Mary."

Mary laid her darning in her lap. Her lips clamped back words.

"No need to say anything, Mary. No need to say words you'll regret. I forgave Father years ago, even if he was a little delayed in forgiving me."

"But...how did you hear...the newspaper?"

"No. He sent for me yesterday in the morning."

"Oh, John...he...he wanted to see you?"

"Yes. Poor old duffer. Been wanting to see me for years. Just didn't know how to do it."

"What did he die of, John?"

"Hardening of the heart, Mary. Not his arteries, like Mama; his heart. Oh, actually, he'd had pneumonia some time back, and never quite recovered. Said he'd lain there in bed, thinking things over, and wanted to make a new start. The doctors could find no real cause of death. It was quite pathetic, really. He planned all sorts of things we could do...together. Even asked to see Jessie...and the child."

"Did they come?"

"No. That's my other news. Jessie divorced me a while back. I would have written you, but I wanted it to be final. I couldn't quite believe it myself. Funny thing, she was married only the day before yesterday to another man. Oh, I can imagine the state she's in, missing a chance at the money by one day." Drops of bitterness, like sweat, had come into his voice.

William Jewell slapped his knee with his pipe and guffawed, then slunk back into silence. John got up and paced the floor.

"There's something I have never said to any human soul, and shall never say again. But I'd like to say it now, to you folks. I married Jessica because she told me she was going to have a child by me. Since the day Father cut me off because of it, Jessie has been, as you know . . . well, she has been what she was to begin with, and I without the sense to know it. A harpy. A slut. And worse . . . a prostitute. She went back to her trade the day I started carrying hod for my living. I suppose I was over-proud. I refused to use my name, my incomplete education, to seek any other sort of employment. I wore a hair shirt. I thought, by doing what seemed to me honest labor, of the sort she could understand, by trying to make acquaintance among the people she was at ease with, I could make a woman of her. I don't know . . . I do not know! Perhaps if I had tried a . . . a better-paying job, had given her some money . . . had introduced her among my friends . . . ah, no. Poor pretty child! Cheap little gutter rat!"

"John!"

"Yes, Mary. She was just that. The world is full of people, people we all know, or think we know, well . . . who aren't quite . . . quite normal mentally . . . and morally. Oh, yes, morally. Children and idiots, Mary, have no morals. Jessie had no brains. It might have been better if she had. God knows I tried to help . . . I tried. Christ in heaven, seven years of filth and rottenness . . . of laying bricks for a dirty rag of flesh I'd come to loathe . . . for a child that wasn't mine . . ."

"The child . . . not yours . . . John?"

"Oh, she whipped me with that, too. Aagh . . . I've said enough . . . I can't talk about it anymore . . . I can't help talking . . . I feel like . . . like screaming it out . . . like vomiting the whole stinking mess all over the rug. Did you ever hear me shout, Mary? Well, I want to shout now."

The silence wept.

Out of it rode William's voice.

"Shout, John."

Mary Jewell looked at her husband with astonishment, and saw the look that went from man to man. She saw John collapse into a chair, and thought he was going to cry, and thought it would do him good.

But he was laughing. Not wildly, but a little pitifully, as the blossom of the wormwood laughs, expelling worms. Very simply, he said, "Thank you, Will. I guess that makes us even."

And to Mary: "Father changed his will yesterday. You get the town house, Mary, and all the furnishings. I expect, Will, you'll want to be moving to Beacon Hill straightaway."

A little foolish laughter healed the rent in the seamless garment.

"Chris," John went on, "gets a nice slice for his education. I get the rest. I suppose you're sitting here gazing upon a fairly rich man. . . . Well, why doesn't someone ask what I'm going to do with it?"

"Reckon a man don't ask that kind o' question, John."

"There, you see. . . . I've almost forgotten what decent people are like, Will. Well, I'm going back to school. Oh, I've kept up with some reading, though I'm rusty enough. I plan to rest up until fall and go to Germany and finish taking my M.D. You know, I can't believe it yet . . . I simply cannot believe it. To have my books around me again, to be alone . . . alone, mind you . . . with Hesiod and Plato and Pericletus . . . the lamp and the printed page . . ."

"Oh, John, you'll stay the summer with us?"

"B'lieve I told ye once ye'd come in mighty handy long about haying time."

"Better than that . . . better than that." John Trumbull was pacing the floor again, but his feet had some bounce in them now. "I thought it all out on my way up on the train today. I guess I've had it in my mind for years. Mary, do you remember what I once said about the old house, that it was one of the simplest and most beautiful bits of architecture I'd ever seen? Oh, the chimney won't be difficult to rebuild. Well, Will, do you want to sell me the old buildings, and an acre or two of New Hampshire earth? Not only a place to rest for the summer. A place to grow old in . . . peace . . . and the woodbine on the wall.''

William Jewell looked down the stem of his pipe. ''Calculate we can have that chimney in before haying begins. Rest of the house is in pretty good shape, for its age. No need to ask Mrs. Jewell about it. Reckon she's got the curtains all hung, in her mind. Tell ye what, John; name yer price, and I'll throw in that Jersey heifer old Dot dropped yesterday. Ye'll be needin' some female back to rub, ontil ye bring yerself home a wife.''

''A *wife*. I've had a wife, Will.'' Then, perceiving that William Jewell was having his heavy-handed joke out of a sense of well-being that had been little his the past few years, he smiled. ''Besides, Will, if I ever give another thought to a woman, she will have to possess the beauty and purity of the Trumbull women, and the wit and integrity of the Jewells. And something besides. The patience of a fool.''

''Waal, that ain't Phronie Goss, it ain't. Did that clock strike midnight, Mrs. Jewell?''

Eight

To Christopher Jewell, Judith Duchesne was more myth than woman, the one great lady he ever knew. To him, she stood goddess on his familiar earth. Schoodac District and all that here pertained, root stem and mountain fall, every keep of soul and body on the Brook, were in the shadow she cast, the aura about her head, her footfall in the sun.

She came to Schoodac on an April day. Looking back along the path of years, it seemed to Chris that all that winter had been but a preparation for her coming. It was easy enough, afterward, to see the foreshadowing of her in the advent of Uncle John, but only long, long hindsight brought clearly to his mind the meanings behind the behavior of Big Ed during that winter, his huge elemental figure limned on the background.

That Ed was different, with a subtle magical difference, after the brief and fleeting hour of their childhood together, he knew with the infallible intuition of his sensitivity, his own precocious tentacles reaching out of childhood. And if the winter had been for them a time of joys more intimately shared than before, it brought with it, also, an apartness profoundly felt and profoundly not known.

Much of the boys' time had been spent in the winter woods, logging. One of William Jewell's oxen had died two years before, and he had put a young steer in its place, for nigh ox. Whether by temperament a rebel to the yoke, or because he had been cut proud, he had proved recalcitrant, and William Jewell had sworn to butcher him as soon as he could find another for his place. He never drew his share of the load, backing away from his yoke and pawing the ground, and he was as handy with his horns as the bull in the stall.

Chris and Ed yoked the team up on a morning after the snow had settled in the woodlot, heavy and solid for the iron runners of the big sled. The oxen had been in summer pasture up the mountain, and only the day before had been brought down from Iddo's barn. Chris warned Ed about Husky's horns, but even as he spoke, Big Ed, enchanted with this new creature, was standing beside him in the hovel, stroking his ears and feeding him from his pocketful of oats. It seemed to Chris, even then, that in his voice was a note of firmness that had not been there when he lifted Miss Flanders's horse out of the swamp. He was no less soft-spoken, but his authority had deepened. When the loosed ox turned on him, his horns lowered, Ed laughed, and took one horn in his hand, bringing up the great dark head against his breast. He laid his face against the shaggy one, and led him out. The yoke fell over the beast's neck like a charm.

William Jewell, watching the proceedings, said, "Best take the ox goad, Ed."

But the ox goad gathered dust that winter. Big Ed, slogging along beside the team, let his bare hand lie on the troubled rump, and there was communion between them. Chris had never known his friend to talk as freely as he talked with the uneasy steer.

"Now, tome along, ox. See, the snow's all deep an' white an' soft. It's kind o' lovin' snow this day. Looky, here's where a little fox have tome, in the night . . . his paws run pretty. There now, he's had his breakfast fine . . . thar's drippin' blood along. Like he be fast asleep by now, lyin' turlt up 'longside his wife an' chillen. Now, ox, you pull."

Ed's hand, red and huge, lifted and fell, featherweight, and the ox leaned into the yoke.

All winter, Big Ed had a happiness that was something all alone with him. He laughed aloud, and it was man's laughter. For the first time, Chris felt young beside his friend, felt there was something he didn't know that Ed had found out. Ed loved the woods, the logging, and Chris loved it all, too. The hemlocks bowed under their load of white, the jackrabbit in his ermine suit, the blue spruce trees moving their indigo shadows around the dial of the day, the shining and the wonder. They would come into the cathedral nave, into the silence and the thronging sound, as to some holy place. Then Big Ed, having dropped blankets over the standing beasts, would take the ax helve in his hand, testing the blade that had been warmed on the back of the kitchen stove. He would walk around his tree, asking its permission for death, the sound of a little dirge running in his throat.

Then, suddenly, as if a demon had got hold of him, he would back away, let out a scream of joy, and with three terrible whacks fell it between two saplings. These were the moments, interlinear, when Christopher, standing away, felt the drip of the melting noon snow on his face from the branch above, and a little terror blew.

One tree, Big Ed would not consent to fell. A great white birch it was, standing hard by the sled track. William Jewell had marked it for stove wood. The tree was a favorite with Chris. He had known it all his life, and had dreaded the coming of the day when his father would declare it ripe for the ax. Its full white body leaned so that, in passing, the oxen, tipping their horns, had left a scar on the bark. Mary, out gathering arbutus in the spring, called it the Lady Tree. Its white belly thrust tenderly, inviting the palm, and Chris had long had a fancy that one day he could enter there, could just walk into the scar and refuge would be his.

It seemed as if Big Ed knew every tree to be felled before he saw William Jewell's blue chalk mark on it. This one he stood before one morning, rubbed the chalk away with his coat sleeve, and passed along. Chris grieved. This one he would have to take down, then, himself. He put it off, but knew that would be no use. One morning when Ed and the team started off a jump ahead of him, Chris purposely lagged behind, his ax in his hand. He stood by the tree, dreaming, remembering, faint from dim, hurtling hells. He heard Big Ed coming back, and the snarling of The Dog. He had never seen his friend angry before, but was glad.

At suppertime, sidling against his mother at the stove, he told her what had happened.

Mary Jewell waited until her husband had his bellyful and had lit his pipe.

"That white birch, Mr. Jewell," she said.

"Waal, what about it?"

"Would you mind, very much, if the boys saved that one . . . for me? I've always . . ."

"I calculate that tree's ready to come down, Mrs. Jewell."

"I see . . . I see. Well, I guess you'll have to do it yourself, then." She spoke of it, as she seldom spoke to her husband, tolling her own bell, whose tongue lay most often in womb-soft silence.

William rose and knocked ashes against a lifted stove lid. He went to the barn. He had not answered. He did not speak of it again. The tree was not cut that year.

Soon the old hand-coopered buckets of maple sugar stood on their shelf in the cellarway. The first robin was seen. The Brook overflowed the meadow, suckling the roots of cowslip and sweet flag. Sweet rain fell, fragrant on the warm air, and the clouds fleeced out their wool, imitating lambs at eweing time. From under the ragged patches of snow, where the shorn white beast crept away, mayflower buds opened in dew-burst loveliness, fresher than the world's morning, evidence of grace. Lavender and rose and yellow, everywhere. A bluebird sat on a twig and called the sempiternal song of the egg.

Christopher slogged behind the harrow, breaking up the field across the road for planting corn. It was a perfect day, and sweat trickled down his legs as he dreamed of the fish up in Iddo's lily pond. Worm in the furrow, violet in the run, drum and fife of spring. The strike of hammers on nails, where Uncle John's house was near ready for living. Bare feet in the earth.

For weeks past, the goings-on at the James Jewell place had had them all in a knot of excitement. A dozen men had come up from Boston, and the big house stood in a garment of fresh paint like a bride. Rags and buckets and soft soap had been borrowed from Mary Jewell for the scrubbing, and doors and windows stood open for the first time in many years. Eben Peaslee, fetching wagonload after wagonload of boxes and crates, came in now and then for a cup of coffee between trips, or to ask help with an uncommonly bulky or awkward object. Everything was securely boxed, and each item was marked in large black letters, NOT TO BE OPENED. The only clearly identifiable object was the grand piano, and, quite unexpectedly, Uncle John volunteered to help with that. The crate bore the brand name of one of the finest instruments made in the world, and John marveled at its appearance in Schoodac.

"You will like that, won't you, John? To have music?" Mary asked.

"If it's the sort of music that piano deserves," was John's mistrustful reply.

Chris heard buggy wheels on the loose planks of the bridge. He watched a pair of checkreined bays come to a halt. He was close by the stump fence, no more than a few rods from the gate of the big house. He saw Raoul Duchesne hand his wife down before leading the team into the barn.

She stood and looked about her. A light winsome breeze caught the plumes in her handsome hat and moved her long full rich skirt around her thighs. For a moment she gazed at the house. Then a robin in the elm poured down a welcoming melody, and she turned, facing Christopher's way, her head lifted. She did not seem to see him. His horses had come to a standstill, and he made no effort to turn them. He had never seen anyone like her; he had never really seen a woman before. She reached up her arms with a lovely gesture and unpinned her hat, and he saw the dark tower of her hair coiling, coiling around her upflung head. He saw her smile. He saw, for the first time in his life, under her tight bodice, the single most beautiful line of which all art, all nourishment, all meaning, is but translation, of which the swell of the seas and the chiseled valleys of the earth are only broken rhythms of echo, the ineffably desirous, the breast and belly of a woman.

"Gosh," he said to no one, and clucked his horses up.

At dinnertime there was a good deal of talk about John's house, about planting time, and the lambing ewes. Wedges of hot mince pie had been placed on scraped plates before Chris dared to speak up.

"They've come," he ventured, more or less in his mother's direction.

"Yes?" Mary Jewell smiled as though she knew what he meant.

"To the old Jim place."

"Waal, why'n tarnation didn't you say so?"

"I just did."

"Did ye git a good look at 'em?"

"We were just there by the sumac, 'cross the road. He's no more'n a shrimp side o' her."

"And her?" Mary heard something new in her son's voice.

Chris hesitated, blushed, dabbed his fork into his pie.

"She's tall. Her clothes . . ."

"Yes?"

"Well, they ain . . . aren't . . . they're pretty tony. She had great big feathers, kind o' red, on her hat. They looked . . . pretty . . . on her. Aw . . . I dunno."

John Trumbull said, "Let the boy eat his pie."

And William Jewell commented, "Waal, one thing's sartin, he ain't no Jewell. Mebbe she's got Jewell blood in her. All the Jewell women be big."

Chris's voice was a whisper under his chin. "She's...she's different."

Nine

THREE days later, Uncle Bart having reported at dinner that curtains had been hung, Mary Jewell put on her best black bombazine, gathered a handful of violets and lilies of the valley, and went over to call on her new neighbor.

As is the way with all of us, she had made an image of Judith Duchesne in her mind. A woman, perhaps her own age—a little older, possibly; likely as not handsome, so as to have impressed young Chris, but that might well have been only because of her dress and manner. To these conjectures she added her own wishfulness, that her neighbor be neighborly, pleasant to have just over the wall beyond the silver birch. That the Duchesnes would be kind she assumed out of her own innocence of ill will. That they would be company for John stood foremost among her wishes.

It was four of the afternoon clock when she lifted the old iron knocker on the front door. She stood, a tiny compact of gentility and ready heart, the light of loving-kindness on the golden strands of her hair, and heard footsteps.

Nothing had prepared her for Judith Duchesne. For a long moment she had to depend on her smile and her bouquet. But the smile that answered hers was, she thought, the loveliest she had ever seen.

"I am Mary Jewell, your next-door neighbor. I know you must be busy, getting this big house settled. But I thought we should get acquainted, living so close."

"Oh, how good of you. How very kind. And how sweet... how sweet the flowers. Come in. Come in. You will excuse the house."

"Why, my child, I had made you out an old lady, and here you are, nothing but a girl."

A shadow, Mary Jewell thought, passed over her neighbor's face. "Twenty-seven is not a very young girl. And sometimes, too, I feel quite an old lady. Do take that chair by the window. My robin is due for his evening song, and he hurls it right into that window. I think he tries to tell me about his nest and his mate, though he seemed angry at first."

"Do you know what we think he says? Listen... here he is. 'Kill 'm, cure 'm, give 'm physic.' Hear?"

"Oh, he does... he does."

Her laugh was, if it were possible, more beautiful than her voice. Like the old well where the star sat night and day, deeper than depth, forever a star, reflected. She was dressed all in white, and spider-web lace, handmade, ruffled around her slender wrists and at the throb of her fair white throat. Her hands, lying composed in her lap, were strong things, alive in their serenity, and her noble head bore a great burden of braids so that, sitting, she was a tower.

But few would have seen her face as Mary Jewell saw it. It was not a face to describe, to circumscribe with nose and mouth, and frame with ears. It was not pretty. It was not even beautiful, yet. It was remarkable, and Mary Jewell never rightly saw it after that first moment, so soon did it become for her the face of her election, to be cherished and defended.

"But here I sit," she said, "forgetting everything. And the water boiling for tea."

They sat over delicate bone china cups and thin buttered slices, and the robin sang his ludicrous lullaby over and over and over. They heard the rubber tires of a buggy wheel up to the barn.

"My husband," Judith Duchesne said, in such a way that Mary

thought she had not meant to say it. She saw her new friend straighten, felt a quiet shock of rigidity.

Raoul Duchesne came into the room like a cat, like a well-groomed tomcat. He flung his gauntlets on a chair, and bowed from the waist when presented. He strode to the sideboard and poured himself a draft from a decanter. He stroked his waxed moustaches and rocked from heel to toe. His eyes, like lizard eyes, seemed to lock wherever he looked.

"Mrs. Jewell is our nearest neighbor. Her husband's family built this house. She has been good enough to call to . . . to . . ." Judith Duchesne's hands had put down her cup. They were still on her lap.

Her husband's voice cut with a delicate ice of politeness. "We must be content with being grateful, Mrs. Jewell. However, my wife is not well. I have brought her here to be by herself. She will have her household tasks . . . her music. I must be away much of the time, on business. I must ask that she be left alone. Mrs. Duchesne does not require other company than my own. You will kindly convey my wishes to any . . . any other well-meaning natives who would intrude. You will excuse me now."

Mary heard the stamp of heeled boots, like the echo of those incredible words, as Raoul Duchesne mounted the stairs. She said, "Is this your own wish, my child?"

Judith's head was high. It did not move, neither lifted nor lowered, but her eyes met Mary's.

"Then you may tell your husband, if you wish, that I shall do nothing to further his command. What he has to say, he must say for himself. Now, my dear, I must go home and get my menfolks their supper."

They stood on the front porch. The great newly painted pillars were like replicas of their mistress.

"There's no need to explain, my dear," Mary said. "Perhaps I already understand. Remember that my house and home are always yours. And I shall come back . . . only so I do not further hurt you." She touched her palm to Judith's clasped hands. "There are only a few of us . . . and we are kind. You must do only what you think is . . . is good. But you must rely on us."

"Waal, Mrs. Jewell. I see you've been out callin' this afternoon."

"Yes, Mr. Jewell. Will you kindly pass the potpie, John."

"Come, come. How'd ye make out?"

"I took a great fancy to her." Mary laid a careful emphasis on the pronoun.

"An' him? What'd ye think o' him?"

"I wasn't much taken with his manners, Mr. Jewell."

"Manners . . . manners. You an' yer manners, Mary Trumbull."

"There is such a thing as common decency, Mr. Jewell."

"Come, come. Don't tell me he insulted you, first off."

"No, Mr. Jewell. He insulted her."

*T*en

M ARY JEWELL told none of her neighbors of her experience. She pondered the likelihood of Judith Duchesne's being sick, but she was, herself, too widely acquainted with the face and gesture of illness, its colors and all its moods, to think of her friend, for so she thought of her, as being anything but an extremely healthy and uncommonly strong young woman, physically. There was always the possibility that she was recovering from a nervous illness, and this was somewhat supported by her troubled eyes, by the shadow that passed and recurred. But Mary had instinctual knowledge exceeding that of most women, and with all her Christian effort to justify the position of Raoul Duchesne, she simply did not believe the argument of bad health. She simply did not believe in Raoul Duchesne. As a force for some unintelligible evil, yes; as a flesh-and-blood man, no, he had no existence.

After a good deal of thought, she told John her story. It was better, she knew, to leave William in ignorance. His Yankee pride would put his dander up, and that could lead to unpleasantness. But she could trust John.

"I have made up my own mind, John," his sister concluded. "The girl is in trouble. Oh, I shan't interfere, not to be defiant . . . not openly, at least. But I shall watch. Oh, John, he just makes me shiver to think of him. Those eyes . . . cruel. They seem to be . . . well, just staring inside of him. They don't even look through you. I could stand that. And never right at you. They aren't even cold. Coldness is something I could understand, too. It's just as if he hadn't any eyes, John. I don't believe the devil *has* eyes."

Trustworthy John had listened carefully. "Mary," he said, "you're the most percipient person about people I have ever known. If you say she's worth the watching, we will watch her, you and I."

"I know what I'm going to do, myself. He says he has to be away on business. Well, the minute I know he's away, I'm going over again. I'll make some excuse. She wants some roots of my lily of the valley: I shan't ask her a single question . . . you know I know better than that. I'll just . . . keep watch. I knew I could count on you. We'll not tell another soul. They'll find it out soon enough. Phronie's going to call tomorrow.'

Eleven

THE Grange held its regular quarterly meeting the following week, and there were readier tongues than Mary Jewell's there.

Business was got quickly out of the way for this heavier matter. The nights were still cool, and a fire had been built in the big-bellied stove. The ladies, fluffed up amongst their ruffles like setting hens jealous of the secret of the egg, bent over their seams and crochet work. Needles, flying, pricked at the light from the kerosene lamps, dancing in brief, winged arcs, like grasshoppers in passage.

Phronie Goss had made her call. Raoul Duchesne had opened an account at Clessie's store, and had had a conversation with Happy Tandy, the postmaster. Even the menfolks were eager to talk.

Phronie, ever ready to sacrifice her pawn for position, led off. "Waal, she come to the door an' you coulder knocked me down with a feather. I declare, I ain't never laid eyes on a nicer woman. She ain't exactly . . . waal, not pretty. Handsome, I guess you'd call her. An' sweet. My, but she's a lady, too. I declare, I jest like to watch her move around, so dignified like. An' that parlor! Tony ain't the word for it, no sir. Them curtains, why they muster cost a fortune. An', my, you'd a thought I wuz the queen. 'What do you take in your tea, Mrs. Goss? One or two lumps? A slice of lemon, perhaps?' An' me watchin' them white hands o' hers. Waal, I ain't never took any lemon in my tea, but I thought I might's well try it, oncet. Pretty good, too, it were. An' them thin cups! Mercy on me, I was that afeared I'd drop mine I didn't durst drink more'n a few swallers. Nothin' but bread an' butter with it. Like as not she don't know how to bake a cake. Waal, I made up my mind, there an' then, I'd bake one o' my spice cakes . . . but now I reckon I won't."

"Why, Phronie. Why not?"

"I'm a-tellin' ye, Sarah Peavy. Give me time. Waal, we be sittin' there, havin' a good ol' toe-to-toe talk, an' me a-tellin' about you folks, an' all the stories 'bout the Ol' Jim house, an' such. An' admirin' her dress..."

"What was she dressed like, Phronie? I've heared..."

" 'Twas all yellow dimity. Fitted tight 'round her waist." Phronie laid down her crocheting and ran her hands down her skimped breasts. "All tucked and gusseted here. An' a big full skirt, with bitty ruffles, all made by hand. My, there was plenty o' work in that dress. Handmade lace, too. But it's her voice an' her hair that gits you. Her hair comes all the way down to the floor when she's standin', an' I bet she's close to six feet. Gives her trouble, too, her hair does. Times she has to let it right down, the heft on it's too much. An' her voice...it's *that* low, an' kinder soft, too."

Phronie folded her hands and thought for a minute, an unwonted tribute.

"Git along, Phronie. I hear you saw him, too."

"*Saw* him! I saw him all right. Waal, as I say, we wuz havin' a lovely time. An' in he comes. Oh, butter wouldn't melt in his mouth, first off. Made a bow...lawsy me...that bow! But then he didn't hardly give me time to say 'Howdy-do.' Throws them gloves o' his halfway 'cross the room, an' pulls out a gold watch outer his pocket, an' looks straight at her...if it kin be called lookin'. Snake eye, that's him. 'Twarn't more'n four o'clock...mebbe a mite...you know how 'tis...talkin' an' all. 'It's time,' he says, 'for my wife to prepare my dinner.' An' he stands right there while I git up an' go. I warn't minded to budge for no persnickety little shrimp with wax on his whiskers, but she don't say a word, an' I guess I know when I'm not wanted."

"Why, Phronie Goss, how ye talk."

"You ain't never heard me tell a lie, Sarah. You ain't."

"I believe you, Phronie," Clessie Peters said in unexpectedly angry tones. "I coulda thrown him outer the store. Came in askin' for a roast of beef. 'Prime ribs,' he said, as if I was a flunkey of some sort, orderin' me around. 'Six-rib standin' roast,' says he. I told him I'd jest about haf to cut up a whole crittur, fur that. 'Well, cut it up then, my good man.' My good man! Godamighty, that voice. Oh, yes, like you said, Phronie, he's all butter one minute, an' next, his voice is like a ripsaw going through a knot. I allowed as it would cost him somethin', cuttin' right into the middle of a beef like that. 'I didn't ask you about the cost, did I?' he says, an' brings out a fistful of twenty-dollar gold pieces from his pocket. So I got down the beef an' cut his roast for him. Well, he takes one look at the meat, an' says, 'How long have you had that creature?' Well, you folks never had a tough piece of meat from me, not lessen it's the tough parts. I was just about to tell him to take his trade somewhere else, but I didn't. I told him the crittur come right up from Boston the day before, an' that's the truth. An' what does he say to that? 'Well, then, it won't be fit to eat for another three-four weeks. You hang that roast,' says he, 'until I come for it.' An' out he marches. I don't rightly know why, but I could of gladly hung *him* on that hook. I guess some folks like their meat ripe, but it was his way of sayin' it. 'S if he owned my store . . . an' me. I ain't hankerin' to have no more to do with that customer.''

"Ayah, it's like Clessie says,'' Happy Tandy put in. "Comes inter the post office, a-swaggerin' like he does. Writes his name down on a piece o' paper. All curlycues. Criminy God, straighten out all them lines you'd have a pismire track clean to Boston and back. Snap, snap, he goes, like a whip crackin'. Says he ain't ter home a good part o' the time. 'My business takes me away,' he says, pompous as hell. Then he says not to let anyone but himself ever git his mail. Ter hold it until he comes. 'But supposin' there's a letter or a telegram fer yer wife,' I asts, 'an' there's someone goin' over Schoodac way?' 'I'll take care of my wife's mail,' says he, an' I felt I'd been whipped fer so much as thinkin' on such a thing. I swan, I don' know what ter make o' the hull dratted business. Guess we might's well leave 'em be, that bein' the way they want it. Guess we've got along so fer without 'em. Fer myself, I kin stand it ef I never set eyes on 'im again.''

Phronie sat right up. "Waal, that's all right,'' she said. "But I can't help feelin' sorry for her.''

Mary Jewell said, gently, "He told me she wasn't well. That she wanted to be alone. No. He didn't say that, and I won't pretend he did. He said he wanted her to be left alone.''

"You and yer close mouth, Mary Trumbull Jewell,'' Phronie said. "You ain't said a word 'bout even seein' him.''

"Well, I did. And that's what he said.''

"Ast me, she looks strong as a horse,'' said Phronie. "An' tell me this. If she's ailin', how'n the wide world is she ever a-goin' ter take care o' that great barn o' a house?''

Prudence Peters looked up from her stitching. "He's asked Sarilla to go there to help. Three days a week.''

"Sarilla!'' Several voices at once. "Sarilla!''

The needles were exclamation points, bright with incredulity. They pricked the pincushions of the mind, halted and reversed, and leapt up again.

Sarilla Beane. Down there by the railroad tracks. Sarilla, who seldom ventured even into Clessie Peters's all-kindly ken. Sarilla, with a face too ugly to look at, and a great pendulous wart hanging from one chin, a phallic birthmark from which women averted their eyes. Sarilla, who bore the stigma of illegitimacy, too proud to allow Doc Sanborn into her shack. Indeed, since her mother died when Sarilla was sixteen, no one had been inside her tiny house. Every other year, in spite of her corpulence, Sarilla painted her house a snowy white, erecting her own scaffolding and laying on the paint with expert hands. Cinders and soot blew her way twice daily when the trains passed by, but her daisies were whiter than Prudence Peters's, and her garden the envy of every flower lover in all the country round. Her little orchard bore the finest fruits, and in winter the star of Bethlehem shone from her kitchen window, purer than the new-fallen snow. The Beanes were one of the oldest families in New Hampshire, and Polly Beane, Sarilla's mother, youngest and fairest bloom on the old tree, had wandered away into the woods one day, escaping her bitter and stern old father, and met with an experience the nature of which she had never dreamed. What would have happened if old Eliezar Beane had not died before the evidence of Polly's long stroll into life had begun to show, folks often wondered. But

Polly had much of the shrewdness of her forebears, and she realized on her patrimony, keeping only for herself the scant hillside by the railroad tracks, and ensuring for her child a meager income for life. Her ugly duckling she loved beyond human endurance, and when she died quietly in her bed one day, from no apparent natural cause, there were those who said it was God's punishment. And there were a few, at that late hour, who admitted themselves guilty of having ostracized her.

Folks tried to be kind to Sarilla, and their efforts were rewarded by a courteous acknowledgment, and withdrawal. She spoke well and softly, for the Beanes were a bookish clan, and it was whispered that she talked to her cats in Latin. Someone had discovered that she could wash and iron a delicate, many-ruffled garment as could no other woman in town, so a few took their washing to her door. One mystery about her had never been solved. Years ago she had let it be known that she would be glad of any rags of any sort that folks would be kind enough to give her, and she might be seen, almost any fine day, a grain sack over her shoulder, collecting her sack of old clothes and odds and ends of leftover stuffs. What she did with them, no one knew, but there were few rags in the countryside that did not go into her clean ragbag. Oh, she was clean. Her old mother hubbard was immaculate, and the ragbag itself was ironed. In the time of spring housecleaning she could be seen scrubbing the under side of the floorboards of her small porch. There was, too, much curiosity about her personal wash line, for there could be seen delicate undergarments, fit, they said, for a queen, along with the rags she gathered hung out in multicolored array. That house, folks reckoned, must be stuffed to the attic with bright bits of useless materials. But why? Why? Well, there was a strain of bad blood in the Beanes, and Sarilla's mother hadn't helped it any. Gathering rags was harmless enough. The women gave her only those left over from rug-making, and she took their second-best with a courteous smile, which made her face, in spite of rather fine eyes, uglier than ever.

And how on earth did Raoul Duchesne coax Sarilla Beane to work in the big house, even for two or three days a week?

"Sakes alive," said Phronie, "it ain't as if she took stock by money.

Sally Winters says it's as much as she can do to make her take a penny for her wash. Anyways, she was left well-off enough. Hm, beats me."

Prudence said, "Well, there's one thing Sarilla can't resist, as you all know, and that's a sick woman. I declare, she was an angel, that time Clessie's mother was so sick. An angel. Poor soul, I guess we've neglected her, though goodness knows, it's hard enough to do anything for her."

"Waal, maybe that's it," Phronie begrudged. "I must say, though, Miz Duchesne's able to git a good wash on the line every day. Them starched white shirts o' his. An' clean underdrawers. An' white lawn nightshirts. An' starched this, an' starched that. It's a wonder she don't haf to starch his pisspot fer him."

"Now, Phronie Goss," Willie Pike spoke up. "Jest because Godamighty put your bladder where yer tongue oughter be . . ."

"Shucks, I don't *care*. I'm downright sorry for her, like I said. I can't quite make it out, but spite o' her laughin' an' all her sweet ways, suthin's eatin' that girl."

Homely old Nellie Perkins found the courage to speak. "Mary," she said, "you've seen her plain. What you got to say?"

Folks didn't ask Mary Jewell's opinion unless they wanted the straight of the matter.

"I am much taken with her," she said, counting stitches in the sock she was knitting before laying the work in her lap. "Some way, ever since that day he put me out of the house—oh, yes, Phronie, he plain asked me to leave—I've had in mind the sermon Parson Wiggins preached at meetin' Sunday before last."

"Why, Mary, it were all about jealousy. Now, let me see. The text. 'Twar kind o' funny."

" 'At the gate of the altar, the image of jealousy,' " Mary quoted.

"Land o' goodness, Mary," Phronie said, slapping the air with impatience. "Fer's I know, ain't one on our menfolks set eyes on her yit. You ain't sayin' he's jealous o' a lot o' old women like us?"

"No, Phronie. Jealous of her."

"Fer pity's sake, Mary. Times, I think yer a little off in yer head yerself. I reckon it's time fer a cup o' coffee. You got that kettle boilin', Nell? Come on, ladies. These menfolks is slobberin'."

They were picking the crumbs from their clothes when the door creaked slowly open, and Sabina Dow came in.

A wisp, she floated by and sat herself cross-legged on the floor by the stove, where the glow from its isinglass door smacked her face with the red smoulder of doom. On every face dread darkened, and plain-visaged fear. Who? Who now? They all heard the soft rising wind flow like a river in the silence, and an old owl echoed their question from the chestnut tree out back: Who? Who?

Sabina looked at no one. Her old old eyes were bright, and her voice as gosling down, speaking the tongue of Leftenant Fitzwilliam Dow's wife, that none fully understood, but all rightly guessed.

"Ay, blatherskite," she said. "Ar coom ahint her back and blether, blether, blether."

Only Phronie ever talked back to Sabina, not holding with second sight. "We jest be a-speakin' o' Miz Duchesne, Sabina. Ain't no harm at that."

But Sabina had wandered off up air, where Phronie's words had in them neither reach nor fetch. Only the settling of a stick of wood in the stove was evidence that they still sat on chair and bench in the Grange Hall. Sabina had taken them with her, out where destiny rides up the wind, and evil and the dark and the star.

"Ar be un beauty walkit by un burn. Saft, saft, un beauty gae. Harkit the pousie wind, ca' doon, ca' doon. Hersel' un quean, wi' hair tha' sets her weel, dirkit it flow un bonnie manteel doon. Sair gude, un couthie quean. Ay, owsen an' auld crocks wi' lambs, wee scrimpit birds an' flitterin' things, coom croonit her wanrestfu' heart. An' ye, thae neebors by un burn, whyles mickle stay a-by. I rede ye, stay a-by."

Sabina had risen to her feet. She leaned forward, and whispered huskily:

"I ken auld hornie, bum an' breek, be at her heel. Ye mauna let him whang. Yestreen I kent a bizzard bird, wi' great gloves yaff an' yerk.

Thae mon, thae mon! Ochone, rive weel thae mon, auld bizzard bird. I shanna let-a-be. Fegs! An' I drink doon his blude, I shanna let-a-be . . . I shanna let-a-be. Ca' up thae wind, ca' up thae wind. A hunder year I walkit on yon burn. Ar mony whyles I catch auld hornie by his tail. Waes me, I'se auld an' auld an' auld. No mair alone ha' I thae power my braw father put-a-me longsyne, longsyne. I rede ye, neebors, stay-a-aby."

She wafted down among them, touching each as though a benediction and an oath befell them all, and chanted:

"Ane cooms. Himsel', he coom an' yerkit at auld hornie's tail. I ken him mony days by yonder burn. An' wi' him yon great bawtie gowl. Ha-step-an'-loup, he follow her. Harkit thae song on gloamin' time. Lee doon, lee doon, ye crocks wi' lamb. Lee doon, yon owsen i' yon stall. He fetchit unchancie coom."

"Pshaw!" Phronie couldn't endure the silence in which the group brooded on the unchance that was to come to Judith Duchesne. "Ef ye ast me, her hair don't be nothin' but a burden on her head, the heft on it. Gives her them headaches, so's she says there's times when her husband ain't to home, she jest has to take it down, to git some ease."

Sabina came out again from her dark reverie. "Harkit a skirlin' on the night, last equinox. It reelit on the moon. Ar scraitchin' sair, un dog, un man. It ar foretellin'."

"Shucks, Sabina. That warn't nothin' but that foolish great boy they call Big Ed, an' his all-fired big dog."

"Ay. Ar foretellin'."

"Sabina Dow. You're jest talkin' to hear yourself talk. What's that got to do with Miz Duchesne?"

Sabina got to her feet. Thin reed of time, she hung over Saphronia, swaying on her feet like sweet flag in the wind.

"I rede ye, Phronie Goss, let-a-be, let-a-be. The scrimpit soul o' ye wanta naethin . . . naethin' at a'. Un here I ken, an' here, an' here." She beat her fists against her head, her breast, her belly. "Yestreen there coom upon the wanrestfu' wind ae bizzard bairn, foretellin'. Thrawn quair, it were, an' unco hungered for fresh carrion. Un flaff un wings, a-flitterin'. Un thrapple tauld o' blude an' death. O' red red blude aside the burnie banks. O' beastie blude an' blude o' mon, an' dree. An' whyles a birdie bairn, whyles brawn great mon, whyles croonin' saft, ar tell un couthie queen, wi' thickened hair wha' sets her bonnie weel, an' winds an' winds, an' fetchit wi'in the toils the bizzard meat. Thar bird, he yerkit at her hair, an' yerkit, an' yerkit. Mickle long it grew on her bonnie head. Mizzled against the moon, it were. An' fetchit adown the burn an' blew an' blew on yonder mountain top. Like milk it were, in shinin', an' murky black thae shadows under thae saugh-woodies whar the willow groaws. An' like it were she walkit sleepin' on the heath, holdin' her hands afore her belly, here, as 'twere her beauty keepin' there, an' she were loth to let it fra its hidin' place. Waes me! Waes me! An' she so cannie sweet an' mickle ado to keep hersel' frae harm. An' whyles I harkit on the could auld wind, the scraitchin' o' the beastie an' the mon, wailin' the moon. Afore my e'en thar bizzard bird waxed fat an' fat an' fat. Un flew agin yon moon, un droolin' blude. Three times un flew an' keckled fit to dee. An' red red blude ar drippit in the burn.''

Sabina was a popple in the April gale rising outside. From her dark thin fingers as she flung her hands in air, Chris Jewell could see the drops of blood, and the great buzzard bird against the moon.

"Ar coom a beauty walkit by yon burn. Ar coom a bitter bane upon yon burn. Ar beauty long foresmitten by mon's rod. Ar still in sleepin' as a bairn, an' yearnin', for un breath. Three winds o' death coom hither on yon moon. Three burthened winds, nor beauty hurts awake.''

There was no sound at all in the Grange Hall. A shutter banged outside, and as if in answer to Sabina's words, the wailing of Big Ed and The Dog could be heard between the breaths of the gale. All within were held, spent with fear, for there was no man present whose life did not in some way touch every other life in the District. Chris, trembling in his corner, resolved that, first thing in the morning, he would go gunning for that pair of buzzards. He already knew where they were nesting: in the top of an old pine up back of the Sawyer place.

The cloak of vision fell from old Sabina's shoulders, and she left the building like a shell emptied of all life, letting the fearful wind clutch at every heart as she opened the door.

Phronie was the first to gather her wits about her "I reckon a cup o' coffee's what we need. Hannah, you go put the coffeepot on. The cream's in that pewter jug on the drainboard. Mercy, someone should take Sabina off down to Concord to the 'sylum afore we all go daft. Now, let's us see. Whar wuz I?"

Peaked little Sarah Peavy took up her sewing wrong end to. "You was acallin' on Miz Duchesne."

"Oh. Ayah. Waal, as I was goin' to say, she do be nice. Spang inter the parlor we went. 'Twas all as tony as you please, with a china teapot as she says her sister from London, England, give her, an' weeny cups, s' thin I like to broke mine from jest handlin' it. Waal, we wuz havin' a good toe-to-toe talk, her an' me. 'Twarn't more'n four o'clock, mebbe a mite after . . . an' the door slambangs open, an' in *he* comes."

The menfolks, glad to be back on the solid ground from which Phronie Goss had not lifted her flat feet, sat up and took notice, even though Phronie was repeating herself. No man in Schoodac District had yet spoken to Raoul Duchesne, and male curiosity was as rife about him as the womenfolks were agape hear about his wife. Some had seen him bustling about when he first moved in, and all had seen him sitting up straight in his new top buggy behind his spanking chestnuts. But the best neighborliness of a New Hampshireman is not to meddle without call for it, and it didn't appear as if Raoul Duchesne was one to call for meddling. William Jewell had been spreading manure on his field across the road when Eben Peaslee had driven up from the depot with a load of furniture, and he had been half minded to go over and offer his help in setting up the kitchen stove. But the way the man had rapped out orders to Eben, in a voice like a whiplash, had put him clean off. Little was known of the newcomer except that he was a Canuck and a horse trader, and that he was off down Boston way a good deal of the time. A small man, always dressed fit to kill in store clothes, he hippity-hopped about, not once lifting a finger to help, and William had no liking for a man who didn't take a hand. He dubbed him Little Dootchy then and there, and the name, fitting him as snugly as those driving gauntlets he never seemed to be without, stuck to him to his death. Long years afterward, it echoes in varying tones of disrelish all over the countryside.

"Fust thing he done," Phronie continued, "war to throw them gloves clean across the room. 'Magine my Bertie litterin' up *my* house like that! He ain't much o' a figger, I c'n tell ye that. Him a half a head shorter'n her, an' twistin' the ends o' that fool moustache he's got. Waxed, I do declare. Waal, she don't bat an eye. Jest keeps on smilin', that sweet way she has, an' innerduces us. Lordy, he wuz all perliteness fer a minit. But them eyes! Cold's a snake's, they be. Stares ye up an' down, like ye be some ol' nag fer swoppin'. I swan, I felt I'd left my petticoats to home.

"So . . . he marches up to the sideboard an' pours hisself a drink o' somethin' outen a cut-glass bottle an' swigs it down. Then . . . wha'd'ye suppose? He takes a gold watch outer his vest pocket an' looks her straight in the eye, an' wants to know, ain't it pretty near supper time."

"You don't say!"

"Why, Phronie Goss, how ye do talk!"

"What on earth'd she say to that?"

"Waal, she don't stop smilin', but I could see she was plain flummoxed. I warn't minded to budge for no man hain't got the sense to grow an honest beard, but 'twas plain to see I warn't wanted. I don't blame her for not speakin' up. She's stuck with him, an' I wouldn't noways answer for what would happen to a body as crossed him. Me, I'd rather get in bed with a' adder, I would. Waal, she comes to the front door with me—I never got a *peep* at the rest o' the house—an' when we're outer hearin, she tries to smile an' says she hopes I'll come agin, often. An', y'know, out in the daylight, like that, I could see that smile was all put on. My, it fair give me a start to see them eyes, all tired like. Y' could see she didn't think I'd come again. An' one thing's sartin, I ain't, onless I know *he* ain't to home."

Chris Jewell, sitting up straight in his corner now, could only think of Little Dootchy, dangling from the rafters of the Grange Hall like a scalded fowl, his last pinfeathers being drawn.

Hannah Mason at last saw her turn. "He was off down to Boston when I stopped in," she began wistfully. " 'On business,' she says. My, but she keeps her house nice, with flowers an' all. How in the world she manages to keep them doilies on the chairs so white, with all the grease they say he puts on his hair..."

Twelve

APRIL passed. Along the verge of the meadow, fern brakes unfurled their tiny clutching fingers, like newborn babes, and the satin faces of the cowslips mimicked the sun. An early golden oriole, bright feather duster on the azure sky, stuffed her beak with threads of sock and woollen underdrawers from Mary Jewell's clothesline, busily fashioning the nest that would hang like a long coin pouch from the bough of the Gravenstein tree and swing like a lullaby in the breeze. The antic new-dropped calves capered in the brash green of witchgrass, their tails held comically straight up, and nibbled round the dogtooth violets along the walls. Sumac and clover leaf and apple blossom, jack-in-the-pulpit and tiptilted robin head, listening for his worm, and all the myriad miracles of resurrection sang out the coming of May across the gentle foothills of New Hampshire.

Ever since Sabina Dow had spelled out her words of doom, Chris had stuck to his friends like a leech. For now he counted The Dog, alongside Big Ed, as a friend. Chris didn't cotton to dogs in general, but The Dog had taken on for him a personality as definite and human as that of his master. There were things about the great black beast that set him apart from other canine creatures. Even with Big Ed he never fawned or curried favor. He had such dignity as few men have; he was seldom seen running. With Chris he was good-humored and protective, but not intimate. A sort of august courtesy marked his attutude toward Mary, and he would accept a bone from her hand with one paw lifted in condescension. He kept a little distance between himself and William, and somehow he seemed to think Uncle Bart funny. With Uncle John he came nearest, with anyone besides Big Ed, to a man-to-man understanding. He would lie upon John's door rock in the sun while Chris and Big Ed got in his wood, and of a Sunday evening after supper, when John came over to the house to read out passages from the Good Book to the assembled family, he would settle himself on the old hooked rug at John's feet, his nose between his paws. He seemed to enjoy the deep, well-modulated voice as it intoned the sonorous rhythms of Ecclesiastes or Isaiah.

"He's the best judge of character I know," John would say, scratching The Dog's ear. "Have you seen him look straight through Phronie Goss, as if she really didn't exist at all?"

No fear of man or event ever showed in The Dog's dark brooding eyes. But he had a fine contempt, and moments of pure animal ugliness unhindered by any consideration of Christian forbearance. On one occasion, Quint Haley had driven into the yard, on some errand from his father. He had put the horsewhip in its socket, and had started to leap out over the buggy wheel, but he turned right around in midair and scrambled back, hearing the snarl that issued suddenly from the barn. So, at least, Chris later testified. It was plain to see that The Dog had no forgiveness in him.

One night early in May, the nigh ox took sick with the pneumonia. William sent down to The Corners for Old Doc Gotchie, but he was off over Derry way and wasn't expected back before morning. There wasn't much you could do for a sick ox, anyway. Like all big strong creatures, once they sickened, they were like to die. That ox had been the last-born of twins and never had seemed quite right somehow.

"It don't look to me the crittur'll pull through the night," William said gloomily as he washed up for supper. "He's wheezin' wuss an' wuss all the while."

Mary was warming horse blankets before the open oven door, her brows drawn together. The loss of a farm animal was not only the loss of valuable property; it was often as close a sorrow as the death of a human friend. The burying ground, down at the sandy foot of the south hang, was scarcely less sacred than the family cemetery.

Chris took his place at table, but he couldn't eat. He reflected that, six months ago, his father would have taken the death of that ox as an act of Providence. He opened his mouth to say something, but thought better of it.

"Eat your supper, son," his mother said gently. "Mr. Jewell, do you think it possible? . . ."

" 'Twon't do no harm. Likely no good, either," William answered gruffly. "Run along, boy, and fetch Ed. He's got a way with that crittur."

Chris was off like a streak of lightning. Many years later, he still loved to tell about that night, sad though it turned out to be. Of Big Ed, sitting on the floor of the stall with the great horned head in his lap. The lantern flickering in the wind that came in through the crannies of the old barn, and the way the cattle lowed and the mare softly whinnied. Betweentimes, you could hear the mice nibbling. The shadows of the barn cats came and went, and now and then a cowflap dropped on the hovel floor. The Jersey bull rattled his nose chain uneasily, and the chaff on the floor whispered aloud.

Big Ed, circling his arms around horn and head, talked as Chris had never heard him talk before. Of the woods in logging time, and the full buckets of sap they'd hauled to the sap house. Of upland summer pastures where a beast of burden took his rest. The Dog lay close by, and that night Chris knew better than to venture too near. Sometime past midnight, the wheezing eased, and Chris streaked it for the house to tell the good news. But when he came back, the shaggy great head lolled to one side, and the tongue hung out. Big Ed, still holding on, was rocking back and forth, back and forth, like a mother with a dead child. He and The Dog were singing a dirge, so plaintive with woe that Chris left them there, stumbled up to bed, and bawled himself to sleep.

For a week, it was useless to try to find Big Ed.

"He don't come home at all," his father said. "I ain't seed or heared o' him. Don't fret yerself, boy. He'll git hungry one o' these days. He allus does."

Chris found Big Ed and The Dog sitting on the kitchen door rock the morning he slipped from the house early in order to gather mayflowers. March had brought blizzards, and April had been far from warm, and patches of snow remained in swampy places in the back pasture. The mayflowers, slow budding, had swelled to heady clusters that lipped the frayed edges of the snow and twinkled in dewy pink fragrance from under moss and ground pine and checkerberry leaf. Chris, who loved a blossom as if it were a gift straight from the hand of God, was torn between two emotions. Delighted to see his friend again, but the one mayflowering expedition he allowed himself during the year was something so intimate and precious to him that, for once, he almost wished to be alone. There was little he did not wish to share with his friend, but the spring morning and the mayflowers called for an almost godlike dedication. He had not known Big Ed to pay any mind to flowers.

Together they trudged in silence up through the blueberry pasture to the lot that had been timbered off a few years back, where the saplings that had been left standing were now lusty young trees, and where frog eggs floated among the spew in jellied masses on the woodland pools. The day was coming warm, and the jays fell in liquid waterfalls of virgin blue out of the leafing trees. Birdsong and undersong of first faint peepers littered the air. Spears of tender checkerberry came shyly up amongst the berries of last year.

By a bed of wet moss at the edge of the old wood road, Chris knelt and pushed away the leaves. Dewy and pink and fragrant the clusters lay, like the heads of tiny babies on their pillow of green. Big Ed also got down on his knees. His pale eyes turned to violet and he placed one palm over moss and flower. Chris could feel his joy as his friend felt the joyous morning. Ed made no move to pick a bloom. Instead he rose suddenly and struck out into the yonder woods.

Chris forgot Big Ed, forgot everything but the rite of mayflowering. Vaguely, he heard the two thrashing about in the underbrush.

Presently Ed was calling: "Tome, boy. Tome over here."

Chris found Ed shoulder high in fallen limb and stump at the far side of the swamp. It took him some leaping from hummock to hummock, some quarrel with blackberry vine and fenny bush, and a pair of very wet feet, to reach Ed's side. There, where he stood, beside a small sloping platter of earth, was such a carpet of white and pink as Chris had never seen. He thought they must have found the best mayflowers in all New Hampshire, a place where virgin vine had overcrept since last year's picking; where the heads of blossom were almost as big as a boy's closed fist, and fresher than the dawn of day.

It was past milking time when they hurried homeward down the wood road. Ed had not picked one blossom, yet he seemed to have them all in the look of his eyes. Chris, though, had picked so many, he could scarce see his way through the birnham wood of his bouquet, his belated Easter offering to his mother. He dreaded his father's opinion of a boy who didn't know when an udder was full, but it was worth going without his breakfast for, worth a whole day of getting out manure, his likely punishment.

William was just getting up from the table, wiping his beard with the back of his hand. He fixed the boys with stern eyes. "Where in tunket you been traipsin' off to all the morning?" he demanded to know. "Them cows don't milk an' fodder themselves, you young ape."

But Chris had seen the milk pails on the drainboard, and the milk already setting in the pans. His mother, smiling over her bouquet, patted him on the shoulder.

"Your father and Bart have done the chores," she said, "and your father thinks . . ."

"Water's down in the Brook," William said, and his eyes had an uncustomary twinkle. "Reckon I feel a hankerin' for a mess o' trout. You done good work in sugarin' time, you and your helper here. Git some vittles inter ye an' be off. Best fix 'em up a mite o' dinner to take along,

Mrs. Jewell. Hear tell they's mighty big fish up in Iddo's lily pond.''

This was the kind of moment a boy never forgets. To have earned from his father the utmost of compliments, that he had done good work, was itself bounty. But a whole day off! When he had expected a dressing down!

The day was unseasonably warm, and the trout, feeling the first real warmth of the year, were greedy for fat worms. The boys ate their baked bean sandwiches high up on Kearsarge, and found a few wild strawberries half ripened in the lee of the mountain. They stripped and swam in the pool by Uncle John's meadow on the way home. Tired and ragged and happy, they cut across the meadow, gathering a mess of cowslip greens into their discarded shirts as they came. Until they came up to the barnyard fence, they paid no notice to the moaning of the cow that stood inside.

She stood there, whipping her backsides against the bars, and her keening was an agony to hear. The points of two tiny yellow hooves protruded from underneath her tail, and the sweat of her travail darkened her chocolate flanks. Uncle John stood by, running his hand over her neck and talking to her.

Big Ed dropped his string of fish to the ground.

"She always calves hard," John said. "But she has the best calves of them all. Come on, old girl. Try again."

Chris had never seen Big Ed act the way he did. A kind of excitement quivered all over him. He went up to the cow, and began massaging her along the belly, rubbing the sweat away, and his voice had more of human laughter in it than it ever had before. Though he was always deeply shattered by suffering, he now seemed highly delighted.

"Tome on, bossie," he said. "Tome on, heave a bit. Easy . . . easy now, dest take it easy. Whatever's holdin' ye back, little bossie? Don't ye know well it's time ye was born? Now, boss . . . now, boss."

The calf, shining and wet, dropped suddenly. It seemed as if the whole world sang. Up in his tree a robin shouted lustily his vespers: Kill-him-cure-him-give-him-physic . . . Kill-him-cure-him-give-him-phys- ic. The cow, licking away the caul in which the calf had been born, lowed all the tender mother-music of the earth, and the swallows, painting the evening sky with streamers of silver and black, now seen, now invisible, chattered to and from the cupola of the barn. Big Ed danced about, unable to confine his merriment. He ran and got a shovel and tossed the afterbirth over the fence, and fetched a measure of grain for the cow. When the calf struggled to its wobbly legs, he couldn't hold himself in any longer. He picked it up and stuck its nose under the udder and looked on with such pride you'd have thought he'd given birth himself.

John laughed aloud. "I guess he's yours, Ed. That's the first bull calf she ever had. How would you like him for your own? He'll make a first-rate ox one of these days."

Big Ed stood very still. The tears that were always close for weal or woe wetted his cheeks. For this he couldn't find any words, and John required none. Chris, realizing the fish should be cleaned soon, picked up Ed's string and stivvered home, trying along the way to figure out whether Ed would take the calf home to bed with him, or just camp out in Uncle John's hovel for the rest of his life.

The sun went down in a blue pearmain sky, with a clear green underlay and a blush at the blossom end. Over the Uncanoonucs, far to the east, the moon came up. The first whippoorwill etched his clean monologue against the still dusk, and a dreaming mist hung over new-ploughed ground. Chris, weary with the joy of the day, had just climbed the back stairs to bed when he heard Big Ed and The Dog over in the Sawyer field. He changed his mind about bed and slipped out to join them.

They had just got well tuned up for their serenade to night when Chris saw the kitchen door of the Duchesne house open, and Judith Duchesne came out. She gathered up her water buckets and started down the path to the well house. Halfway down, she stopped to listen. Big Ed, his eyes closed, was singing high and glad, a song, Chris thought, of gratitude for the calf. Judith Duchesne stood no more than a few rods away, and the moon struck full upon her. A thin breeze had come up with the sundown, and it billowed her skirts about her thighs, and fashioned the high full line of her breasts in loveliness against the silver background of the leafing birch. She did not dress as other women thereabouts. Her garment, of some fine silk, snugged round her slender waist, and the full skirt, blowing, made shadow and sheening all about her. She had let down her hair, and what was said of it was true. It feathered in the grasses at her feet, and the moonlight, lipping the dark cascade, limned it with quicksilver kisses as it flowed.

To a boy brought up in the workaday world of Schoodac District, the beauty of woman was no more than a phrase, if even that. Even in their go-to-meeting garb, the women of the District and The Corners, handsome though some might be after the manner of matrons, were far from stirring up, in a boy whose glands were waiting on a miracle, the quick response sheer loveliness could give. Minnie Graham, conceded to be the local beauty, was apple-cheeked and familiar. But here was something else, something that quickened subtly in a boy's blood, something that hurt in his vitals, that turned him hot and cold.

" 'Ar be a beauty walkit by un burn,' " Chris whispered aloud.

Big Ed opened his eyes. The song died in his throat. He sat for a long moment, staring, while Judith Duchesne came down the path. Then he tumbled from his perch like one possessed, sloshed across the Brook as if it wasn't there, and took the water buckets from her hands. Chris didn't dare move, and, for one moment when The Dog approached her, he held his breath. It was a wondrous strange thing to see, the way The Dog behaved. He didn't even sniff. He just sat down at her side, as proud as she, and let her scratch his head.

Big Ed must have lugged enough water to her cistern to fill it to overflowing. When he could find no further excuse to fetch and carry, he hung the buckets on their pegs, and came and stood beside her, looking down into her face. Chris was reminded of a statue he had seen the time he went to visit Uncle John, down Boston way. Bigger than life they stood, those three, and motionless as stone.

The sound of rubber tires murmured on loose planks of the bridge down the road.

"Perhaps you'd better go home, now, Ed," said Judith Duchesne.

"Thank you so much."

"What say, ma'am?" Ed muttered, but Chris knew he only wanted to hear her voice again.

But she had turned abruptly and hurried into the house, gathering her hair upon her head as she went. Ed and The Dog sloshed back across the Brook. Ed was trembling from head to foot.

They heard Little Dootchy as he rolled the barn door to, heard the bang of the kitchen door as he went in, and saw him fling his hat and gloves across the room. They could see Judith Duchesne brewing a pot of coffee, her hair wound loosely round her head. They watched as he downed his coffee at a gulp, then walked up behind his wife and slapped her on the buttocks.

Chris felt the crimson mounting in his face. He wondered what his mother would do if his father tried a nasty trick like that. Judith Duchesne stood rigid as a pillar, her hand arrested where she had started to push the coffeepot to the back of the stove.

Big Ed started up, his fists clenched. Chris could feel the shaking all through the great body beside him.

"Let's us git home to bed," he said.

Chris lay wide awake for a long time. He had not seen Ed fight, and he did not look forward to the first time, which seemed much nearer now.

Thirteen

T first sight, it was a divers
assembly that gathered in the sitting room of the Jewells of a Sunday
evening. They were not churchly people, on the whole, but there was an
unspoken sentiment that where two or three were gathered together to
listen to the Word of God, the sweet amity of family was as close to
worship as need be. Piety, in the sense of evangelical hymn singing and
mouthings of hell and damnation, was as absent from the habit of the
house as the teachings of Robert Ingersoll. And if more than a century
and a half had elapsed since the first Jewell set foot in the colony of
Strawberry Hill, the dignity of the Anglican Church, its beautiful
phraseology and living symbols, still set the tone for the Magnificat that
lay within every heart when Uncle John read from the Bible.

Close to the land they lived, and the words of the Old Testament,
coming straight out of the land of Israel and the milk and honey of that
land, went straight to the core of dailiness. By the still waters of the
Brook and over the green pastures of Schoodac, they went on the soles of
their feet. In years of drought they knew the Valley of Dry Bones, even as
the prophet Ezekiel knew, and when they lifted up their eyes, the cone
of Kearsarge Mountain and all the winning foothills that rose toward the
White Mountains were very present help. Their rhapsodies were daily
toil, the shepherding of sheep, the ringstraked cattle browsing under
willow wands, the wise and foolish candles shaping in their molds. The
way of an eagle in the air, the way of a serpent upon the rock, and the
way of a man with a maid were their profoundest mysteries and their
hourly care. And if the name of Jesus Christ was said aloud, it was like
as not by Uncle Bart in the barn, wrestling to mate the Jersey bull with a
reluctant heifer, or sitting on the grindstone seat whetting a cutter bar.

A lordly pitcher of hard cider, with its pontil mark of old Stoddard ware, sat on the worn Chippendale table hard by a pewter jug of milk, and the corn popper was propped against the granite face of the six-foot fireplace.

William, having put on his overalls over his Sunday-go-to-meeting shirt, dozed in his platform rocker, and Mary, in stiff bombazine, her ramrod back against the rungs of her Windsor chair, sat over her needlepoint, reckoning that a seemly Sabbath occupation. Uncle Bart slouched on the horsehair sofa, the light from the candles striking an unholy note of blood red in his Hungarian glass tumbler, filled with the fruit of the apple. On the shelves of the whatnot in the corner, lustre ware and milk glass jostled with odds and ends of souvenirs marked Niagara Falls or Old South Church. Well-worn rugs, hooked and braided, lay like a blessing on the wide footworn pine boards of the floor. Chris sat cross-legged in front of the fire, wielding the poker his Great-Great-Uncle Philip had forged. That spring, Big Ed and The Dog had added their presence to the group.

John Trumbull held the place of honor in his gooseneck rocker on the opposite side of the hearth from William, and the candlelight fell as lovingly upon the Book before him as that of the oil lamps of old Moses fell upon the tablets of stone. John was only thirty that year, but he seemed older. A little gray had crept in along the lines of his temple bones, and his handsome face was softened by a patina of sadness that was neither grief nor grudge nor gall, but the unfinished distillate of all. Restless he often was, reading far into the night, or striking off across country to fish in Winnepesaukee, or taking the milk train to Boston to spend a week in the Harvard library. It was thought that he was writing a book, but John himself never said so.

Mary Jewell had a mind of her own, and she was minded to be neighborly with Judith Duchesne.

"I'll never ask that man to my house if I can help it," she announced to her husband, "but I'm going to stick by her, for it's in my heart she'll be needing a woman friend. There's somewhat behind that smile of hers that bodes no good."

"Mercy on us, Mary Trumbull. You be talkin' like ol' Sabina

herself," William commented. "How be ye goin' to manage it, askin' a woman withouten ye invite the husband?"

"He's away off somewhere a good deal of the time. Gracious, she does all the work around that place. I've heard her splitting wood after dark, as if she was ashamed to be seen in daylight doing the things no self-respecting man would ask his wife to do. I don't rightly know who cleans up the barn after those fancy horses of his, but I can well guess. There was a lantern in their barn the other night when I went out to hang up the milk strainer, and I know she was shoveling manure. Leastwise, he wasn't home."

"I'll warrant you won't git any thanks for meddlin', Mrs. Jewell."

"Perhaps not. It isn't thanks I'm thinking of, Mr. Jewell. He's gone by sundown most Sunday afternoons. It isn't going to hurt to ask her over here, being he's away, and she lonesome for company."

So it was that Judith Duchesne came into the Jewell sitting room one Sunday evening, and made a part of the family group.

There are no manners in any land more gracious than the simple courtesy of a New Hampshireman. Handed down from English forebears, simmered and refined in the hard circumstances of pioneering, bone clean with necessity, in the castle of a man's house and heart the watchword was kindliness. If you accepted a man at all, you took him whole, and he sat down at table to two-tined fork and Indian pudding. No apologies were made.

Just at twilight of a May evening did Judith Duchesne first enter the Jewell home. Little Dootchy had set off for Boston rather late that afternoon. There had arisen in the neighborhood a feeling approaching a certainty that he didn't want her to go anywhere or see anyone. Phronie Goss and Mary Jewell weren't the only ones who had been practically driven from the Duchesne parlor. The ladies of the Sewing Circle down at The Corners had called to ask her to join, and he had told them to their faces that his wife's place was at home and that he wasn't going to have her off gadding with a lot of females. And Sarah Peavy had dragged her husband there to call after supper one night. Little Dootchy had made it so unpleasant for them that they had beat a hasty retreat as soon as they'd gulped down a cup of coffee and a piece of cake.

"By criminy," Siah Peavy had said. "I never see anythin' like it. I know a thing or two about a hoss, m'self, an' you'd a' thought he'd at least be civil in his own house. I dassent look in the direction o' his wife, though she be som'at to look at. Much as told me to my face I didn't know a wither from a fetlock. Funny thing, too. 'Twarn't nothin' you could 'xactly put your finger on. Jest set and gawked at her. Christ, I could o' took a whip to him."

She arrived at the house a little late and out of breath, explaining that she had had to help her husband get ready for his trip. The others were already gathered. Their two o'clock Sunday dinner had left them all replete with roast mutton and pie, and the reading took place in the edge of the evening, before their light Sunday night repast. A chair had been placed for Judith between John and Mary. The fire, for the nights were still cold, chuckled a resinous antiphon, and tallow candles guttered into their sconces.

John stood up promptly on her coming, and even William, who wasn't much given to what he called citified manners, lumbered to his feet. Chris said afterward that she walked as if she had on skates, gliding. He could see that she was pleased to be there. She greeted each one with a fitting word, and The Dog whimpered with pleasure at her touch. Her lovely tired eyes took in everything. She spoke of the pattern of a rug, the beauty of the old table that was cherished for its long membership in the clan, and tenderly lifted the lilypad pitcher against the light. Big Ed wriggled with delight when she spoke to him, and Chris thought he looked older tonight somehow, manlier. The whole family fell under the enchantment of her voice, even Uncle Bart, who declared later that it had a color in it like goddamned syrup being poured in the sunshine.

When John took up the big family Bible, it opened of itself to the page in which he had put a marker. He had not known she was coming, and he hesitated to begin.

"Perhaps," he said, "our guest would care to select a passage. A favorite psalm, Mrs. Duchesne, or one of the canticles?"

"Oh, no indeed, Mr. Trumbull. Do please go on with whatever you intended. I see you have already made your choice."

"Well, as a matter of fact," John replied, thanking her with a slight nod, "I had chosen something from the Apocrypha. We have been indulging in rather solemn stuff of late, and I thought, tonight, to entertain the younger hearers among us."

"Ah, then. To be sure," said Judith. "The story of Tobit. How delightful, and how fitting! A lad, an angel, and a dog. I know nothing I would rather hear."

"I am a little dubious, madam," John said in his courtliest manner, "about acquainting them with a maid who has been the death of seven husbands. I fear the place will be all cluttered up with the hearts, livers, and galls of all the fish they catch."

Judith's laughter rang about a note of pure merriment.

The reading of the tale was all that could have been desired for the interest of Chris and Big Ed. In it there was fishing, and an evil spirit, and the muting of a little bird dung into a man's eyes. And if they kept their eyes glued to Judith Duchesne's face, and half-unconsciously devised revenges on Little Dootchy for his indignity to this, their queen, they kept their conscious minds on the angel Raphael and his dog, and were enchanted with the little smoke from the innards of the fish that drove the demon from a maiden doomed.

But Mary's mind wandered. She had been right. She was always right, she thought, in such matters. You just couldn't fool her about a woman who was going to have a baby. Show her a girl who was a few weeks pregnant, and her secret stuck out all over her. Not that Judith Duchesne made any secret of it. She sat, oblivious to anything but John's voice, making fine stitches in a long baby dress. When she met Mary's eyes, it was in smiling affirmation, and their friendship, which was to be long, was avowed.

The candles guttered down. Big Ed, urgent for some service, brought in a great four-foot log and placed it carefully on the fire, and for some reason William didn't protest, as he was wont to do, that it would last all night. Perhaps he remembered that Big Ed himself had hewn most of those logs. Mary brought out a Martha Washington cake on one of her best Staffordshire plates, and the boys popped corn over the fire. Over their bowls of popped corn and milk, and wedges of cake piled high with whipped cream, the Jewell family wove Judith Duchesne into the fabric of their lives as though she were the missing thread in the six strands of samite.

After Chris had been sent to bed, and Big Ed home, John absented himself for a moment and returned drawing the cork from a cherished bottle of old port. They toasted their neighbor in old old wineglasses from the top shelf of the china closet, and the silence in which they sipped was far louder than any speech could have been to declare the concord of this meeting.

By the time Judith Duchesne gathered her things into her reticule with the roses of Damascus on it, laughter and peace had wiped the weariness from her eyes, and an ambience shone on her pale face. Her deep voice was husky with tears as she stooped for Mary's good-night kiss.

"Come often, child. As often as you're free."

"Yes . . . yes. As often as I'm free." No further words were needed for understanding.

John had risen when she rose. Taller than she by scant inches, his slenderness seemed somehow to tower over her.

"It will be my pleasure to see you to your door, Mrs. Duchesne," he said.

If she hesitated for the space of a breath, her acceptance was all the more gracious for it. "That would be very kind of you, sir."

Fourteen

THE summer of 1883 came in snorting and pawing the ploughed ground and billowing all over the heavens. Chris smelled a storm when he tumbled out of bed before sunup one morning. By the time he got around to feeding the hens, with the first fingerlings of the rising sun coming through the Uncanoonucs, the old biddies in full feather had spread their wings to catch the very thought of moving air. A robin, yanking at a worm by the door of the chicken coop, stopped with his beak open, as though it was too much effort. The silver edges of thunderheads, up over Iddo's barn, mounted higher and higher, and turned to bronze at the heart.

Sudden and brief, the rain came down the Brook. When it was over, the mercury, which had been mostly in the forties for a month, had blandly climbed up to ninety-nine; and summertime put on her dappled mother hubbard, rolled up her sleeves, and went to work. Sweet and sly, the spears of corn came out in bright excaliburs in the long rows over the stump fence across the road, and out of the exultant earth the pole beans pushed, breach presentation, warming their yellow bottoms in the yellow sun.

Now came the long months when a boy of fourteen on a New Hampshire farm put his nose to the grindstone of hard work. Barefooted and sweating over hoe and scythe, there would be little time for loafing until the hulling and the threshing were done. After the ploughing, when Big Ed could walk behind the plow and wheedle the workhorses into twice their usual stint of work, he took little interest in the farm. The day he tried to help Chris hoe corn, he hoed half of it under and had to be stopped. Once or twice he went out in the dawn with Chris gunning for crows, but he was no help. Killing he just couldn't understand. To him a potato bug was a fond little thing. William found him one day gathering them into a five-quart lard pail, and spoke approvingly of it at dinnertime, only to discover later in the day that every bug had been put carefully back on the ground at the end of the row to begin all over again.

Berrying was another thing. It wasn't that Big Ed loved to eat his pick, for he didn't seem to care much about eating anyhow. Mary worried some about this. A boy that big should have a stomach like an ox, she thought, but John, who took a great interest in the boy, assured her that when a man grew all out of size like that, there were some parts of him that never rightly got their growth at all.

Ed picked his berries out of love. Mary and John would come down to their kitchens in the morning to find buckets of wild strawberries waiting them. To be sure, they were filled with twigs and bugs and leaves, but they were an offering of devotion, even if they did have to be picked over. However, it was Judith Duchesne who got the better part. The first great clusters of wild strawberry, hang-headed on their stems, the first black raspberries from the vines that ran across the little heaps of stones in the hot pastures, the first pale low blueberries, all came like magic to her back door rock.

Judith went rarely to the Jewell house, but Mary took up the habit of running over to Judith's with a pat of homemade butter or a crock of fresh doughnuts whenever she felt sure Little Dootchy wasn't there. Mary wasn't afraid of any man, but she had a nice sense of the situation, and she certainly didn't wish to disturb whatever peace of mind her friend did have.

Judith had never spoken of her husband except in casual reference to his comings and goings. But there was little of the rue and woe of the womenfolks in Schoodac District that did not sooner of later pour itself into the bottomless and armored heart of Mary Jewell. Mary was only thirty-seven that year, but she had early taken her place as mentor and confidante of her little community. For more than a decade, since the death of old Mother Wiggins, she had tied every navel cord, and she had put the finishing touches to every corpse laid out. The running of her gentle voice over the sickly child, the cup of peppermint tea strongly laced with rum for the woman in travail, her hand in the hand of the dying as if she might present him to a friend, were all her lot. She was a womanly woman. Like a great actress, she held her vessel empty for any role she might be called to play.

She found Judith one glittering morning standing over the sink, half in laughter, half in tears. On the drainboard stood a milk pail of blueberries, a two-quart measure of wild strawberries, and a lard pail of the first black raspberries.

"I don't see how I can use them all," she said, a taint of trouble in her voice. "The poor boy! I am so grateful for all his gifts, all his help. You know, he brings up every drop of water I use. Lately, I find my kindling split when I get up in the morning. I...I don't want to ask him to stop, Mrs. Jewell, but the truth is, my...my husband... he really doesn't care for...young people, you know. He...he asked me yesterday where I got all this...and I'm afraid I...I lied to him."

She laughed uneasily, and Mary did too before saying, "There be times, Judith, when what a man don't know won't hurt him any. Goodness, I don't tell Mr. Jewell all I know, by any odds. You just let me take these berries home and put them up for you, and I'll ask my boy to keep an eye on Ed and see he doesn't cause any trouble. If I know menfolks, your husband isn't going to ask where a jar of jam comes from, be there a hot biscuit handy. Now let's you and me have a cup of good strong tea, and you stop fretting. You got somebody besides your husband to think of now."

Mary knew there was much else on her friend's mind than blueberries, but she was not one to ask a personal question. She sipped her tea, and waited. She saw an unmistakable trace of tears around Judith's eyes, but she knew by now that here was a more than ordinary woman, a woman loyal to any vow she took, for better or for worse. As loyal to Raoul Duchesne as she would have been to the best man on earth.

"He...he found out about the baby last night," she said suddenly.

"So?" Mary needed clarification of that remark.

"I guess he had to . . . some time. He's . . . never wanted a child, you know. He . . . he hasn't much patience with them."

"Well, it's time he learned," Mary said with the asperity she saved for downright vexation. "Don't take it too hard, child. Men be a funny lot. I declare, I don't think there's such a thing as a natural-born father, not the way we women are natural-born mothers. I don't recollect that Mr. Jewell ever paid much mind to my having children. He was unduly proud of his first son, and I fancy the good Lord punished him for that. No, child, there be many a thing we women have to bear all by ourselves, many a thing besides our children."

"Yes . . . yes," Judith said, and paused for a moment before continuing. "I suppose I shouldn't talk to you about this, Mrs. Jewell, but he . . . he said he was going to get something down to Boston . . . some remedy of a sort . . . and that I must rid myself of . . . of the child."

"Well, that wouldn't be the first time that's been tried, either," Mary said. "You don't have to take it, you know."

Judith pulled herself together and smiled. "There, I have no right to talk like this," she said.

"Nor have you any right," Mary rejoined firmly, placing a gentle palm on her young friend's arm, "to deprive the world and yourself of the fine children you will have. Why, you are made for having children, lots of them. Just you go right ahead. And don't expect your man to be any help. The poor foolish things, I declare I'm right down sorry for them at times."

Mary went home thoughtfully. She was quieter than usual at dinnertime, watching Chris more critically than ever. After dinner she drew him aside.

"Christopher," she said, "you're growing up now and there are some things you and I can talk about. You're smarter in some ways than other boys your age. You see things. You've seen how Little Dootchy is. Well, he doesn't like to have you boys around the place. I'm vexed as I can be, but there it is. I don't know what the man can do to Ed, but I've a feeling he'll go pretty far to keep him on his side of the Brook."

"But, Mother, far's I know he's never set eyes on him yet."

"Maybe not. It's those berries he brings, and that great stack of kindling he piles up at the door. You keep an eye on him if you can. We don't want his feelings hurt. He's taken such a fancy to her, I can't think what we can do about it. Just watch, I guess, and pray."

Chris didn't know quite what to make of it, either, though he, too, was on the point of idolizing their new neighbor. Each member of the family had his own opinion. At the supper table, William remarked that he'd been in love with his first teacher, and she an old gray-headed lady.

Uncle Bart reached for the cheese. "Goddamn young fool," he said, but affection shone through the words. "Jest don't know enough to keep it to hisself. Jesus Christ, Will, that boy ain't in love, not the way we wuz. He's just clean daft."

John Trumbull held his peace. He spent much time, though, thinking up things for Ed to do, and he almost always enlisted Chris as his agent. So Chris went late up to bed many nights when Little Dootchy was known to be at home, having beguiled Ed and The Dog to go on long treks into the night woods to gather fireflies in a jar, or hunt a screech owl's nest, or just to walk the fields searching out the secrets of the night. But Chris had no real governance over his friend, and had to wrack his brain to think up things that would lure him away. Uncle John was a help, but he had some strange ideas about what would interest a pair of almost-grown boys.

The whole family rallied round. There was, as always in those simple isolated minds, the superstition that somehow the innocent one in their midst had been sent from on high into their care; and where they were hardest to let a normal boy learn to fend for himself, they were tenderest with a lambing ewe or a godsend child.

It was a hot night of late June when Big Ed had his first brush with Raoul Duchesne. Chris had dreaded a little the waxing of the moon, for then he could but follow where Big Ed led. Chris had tramped down six loads of hay that sultry afternoon, and had trudged over Salisbury way to find a lost calving cow before supper, so he had little on his mind but a swim and bed. All day long clouds had threatened a storm, and round and round the horizon the thunder rolled. But the sun went down in sudden splendor, and the triumphant moon marched in serenity upsky.

It was such a night as you know by the touch of things. Chris, who was a feeling fingertip in every part, had had his swim and was lying naked on the ledge. Down his shoulders, the delicate tentacles of the air were like the brush of the beard of young night. The elms, just budding, tapped with velvet knuckles on a damask-smooth sky, and the mist that lay along the Brook echoed the texture of the Milky Way. Chris felt in every pore the growing things. All the billion nostrils of the earth breathed into him the lick and spit of life.

He saw Big Ed and The Dog come down the field and climb up on their rock. He saw the light in the Duchesne kitchen go out, and the one in the upstairs chamber come on. He knew Little Dootchy was at home, because he'd heard him drive in not an hour ago. He knew, too, there wasn't anything he could do about it. He pulled on his overalls, just in case.

The windows of the bedroom were wide open in the heat, and the shades had not been lowered. Little Dootchy must have been already in bed, for he was nowhere to be seen. But Judith came to stand before her mirror, brushing her hair. She wore a white nightgown, made after the pattern of her daytime garments, and the lamplight, falling on her, and the lovely motions of her bare arms, fashioned her into a great white moth with dark wings flying. Her breasts lifted and fell as she moved, and the muted outlines of her thighs could be discerned against the light of the lamp. Chris felt a strange and powerful surge in his loins. He had to do something. He hustled across the Brook to take his place beside The Dog.

Big Ed was tuning up. It came out first in an almost inaudible murmur, like fiddles warming up at a dance. There was no howling at the moon that night, but a new note that made Chris think of the moss roses budding in his mother's garden. It was like the melody of all the soft things that crept on the earth, the wings of all the butterflies and bees, the plaint of the lamb and the singing vireo. Not any song that had ever been heard, but just the sweetest, softest syllables muted into the hot silence of the night. Little cadences of an unearthly joy, honey-pure, rising in volume as the winging of hummingbirds rises in the crescendo of their mating.

Suddenly, like a shot out of a cannon, Little Dootchy was at the window, nightcap askew. His voice slashed out, shattering the music.

"What in hell is that racket?" he yelled.

Chris would have tried to keep Big Ed from speaking, but he was too late.

"It's only me Bid Ed, an' my Dod."

"Well, get the hell out of there, and don't let me hear it again. Do you hear me? Or, by Christ, I'll beat the living tar out of you."

Chris almost snickered at the thought of Little Dootchy trying to beat up Big Ed. But the snicker died in his throat, for he had seen his friend, where other boys or men would have defended themselves to the utmost of their strength, take his great powers all within himself, and weep. Chris, at that moment, began to be a little afraid. He began to feel an unbidden and unpermitted knowledge of Big Ed, and he abruptly knew the truth of Uncle John's statement, which he had heretofore not really thought about, that there were surely some things about a boy who went all to size that didn't grow at all. At the same time, he realized that he didn't know anything about Ed, that there was almost nothing about him that he, or any man, could predict.

The upstairs light went out. In the stillness the boys could hear every sound. The sudden spurts of unpleasant laughter, like the laughter of the menfolks when Willie Pike brought over his stallion and they shut themselves up in the barn with him and the mare. The sound of sharp slapping on human flesh. Stifled, gasping moans that held a meaning any man-grown boy knew only too well.

Chris, still aching in the loins, hung his head in shame. But Big Ed acted like a crazy man. He pounded his fists against the rock until the knuckles bled. His head rocked back and forth as it did when he sang, but this song, if it was one, was not for human ears.

Presently there came from the upper chamber one of the ugliest noises mankind can make. Little Doochy was snoring. Chris said later, if he could have heard himself snoring, he could never rightly have complained about the noise Big Ed and The Dog made. It got off to a spluttering start, with a series of snorts, and gradually worked up to a wheeze and suck, wheeze and suck, wheeze and suck that buzzed at the air like the sawmill that was said to have given Schoodac its name. Schoo . . . dac, Schoo . . . dac.

Big Ed got up and sloshed across the Brook, splashing in all directions as he went. When he reached the other bank, he looked about him as if he didn't know where he was or what he had to do. Chris, watching, shivered with fear. The words to call Ed back somehow wouldn't come. He watched Big Ed go up to the woodpile and start splitting kindling. At first he just hewed splinters, holding ax helve close to its head, shaving furiously. But after a while he clean forgot himself, and began chopping for all he was worth, bringing the blade down with resounding whacks. Chris didn't think Ed was that dumb. He must have known he was making enough noise to raise up the dead.

The snoring stopped. A clatter of slippered feet down the stairs was heard, and the back door flew open.

"For Christ's sake, what's going on out here?"

"I dest be a-splittin' up a mite o' . . ."

Little Dootchy, looking on Big Ed for the first time, stood glued to the doorsill. Ed just stood where he was, foolishly swinging the ax. Little Dootchy backed into the kitchen. Big Ed lifted the ax to begin again, when an iron spider hurtled at his head, and the kitchen door slammed shut.

The spider missed Ed's face by inches, and The Dog hurled himself against the closed door. Ed got him by the ears and dragged him away. Moments later they passed Chris, going straight up through the field toward home.

Fifteen

T HE morning of the Fourth of July
dawned hot and bright. Chris, hurrying up his chores in order to get
ready for the picnic over at Freckle Pond, saw the first streak of the sun
break like a red rosebud out of its chalice of horizon green. It promised to
be a fine day.

In early July there was a brief pause in the farm work. The beans
and corn and potatoes had been hoed and cultivated, replanted for the
depredations of the crows, nursed and prayed over, until now they were
out of swaddling clothes and could be left to sun and rain and the offices
of God. In the toolshed lean-to of the barn, the scythes stood whetted
and ready for the morrow, when the haying season would be officially
ushered in. But today was special: the one day of the year when all the
neighbors gathered together for the annual picnic on the shores of the
lake.

Mary Jewell had taken the bull by the horns, and herself had invited
the Duchesnes. She chose an evening when she knew Little Dootchy was
at home.

"I'm not going to leave her out," she said as she made ready for the
call. "And if he wants to come, that's his business. Anyway, he's no
better than a coward, and I'm not afraid of him."

Instinctively, Little Dootchy knew better than to come to grips
with Mary Jewell. When their eyes met, it was a battle of ill-matched
weapons, for Mary dropped her eyes for no man, and there was
something in their straight steady blueness before which his black, snaky
ones wriggled away.

She could be as sly as the next one, too, when she chose. She put it
up to him directly. "I've come, Mr. Duchesne, to ask you and your wife
to our neighborhood Fourth of July picnic," she said, mincing no words.

Little Dootchy stood rocking on his heels, his legs spread a little wider than was decent. "I ain't never sure when I'm going to be at home," he said, weaseling.

"Then I'll see to it your wife gets there, with us. Everyone goes. We take our dinner and spend the day. It would be a pity to miss it. Folks will expect you to be neighborly."

"My wife goes where I go."

"Well, that's as may be. However, if you can't be here, I'll see to it she comes if she wishes."

"She won't if..."

Mary had her hands folded serenely under her apron. She chose not to let him finish that sentence. "We try to get an early start," she said. "Being as you don't keep any hens, I'll roast an extra rooster. You go straight up the Salisbury road and turn left at the first turning. That takes you right to the pond."

Mary looked every inch a queen, and she managed to make her voice sound like a regal command and a gentle compliment all at the same time. She left the house quickly before Little Dootchy had time to think up anything else to say.

Out of kindness, it was decided to say nothing of the picnic to Big Ed. He didn't like to be where there was a crowd, anyway, and besides, The Dog might prove to be a nuisance. If they turned up, that would be that, they wouldn't be turned away, but even Chris hoped in his bones that they wouldn't.

On the morning of the Fourth, Mary had roasted two of her biggest capons, and packed in the buggy with them were fresh loaves of bread, whole cheeses, a crock of sugared doughnuts, blueberry and dried-apple pies, and one of the Martha Washington cakes for which she was famous. Pats of butter and jars of jam were stowed in the bushel baskets, and a pan of butternut candy for the children. Lemons and sugar were tucked in, and William had wrapped great hunks of ice in gunny sacks, for the lemonade that would be their only drink.

Freckle Pond lay under the northeast lee of Kearsarge. It had got its name from the ring of lily pads that dotted its circumference, and it had a sandy beach as fine as any ocean beach. By midmorning, the folks had gathered from all around, from down to The Corners, and even as far as Henniker and Bradford. Concord buggies, buckboards, hayracks, fringed surreys, all stood in a row at the far end of the beach. The unhitched horses stood tied to trees in the shade, switching flies.

The menfolks stood around and talked crops and haw-hawed at jokes not meant for female ears. The children splashed and swam and yelled. The womenfolk, having whetted their vocal chords on several species of chitchat, were just shaking out their red and white checkered tablecloths to spread on the sand when a smart click of hooves was heard on the road, and the Duchesnes drove in.

"Blessed if he ain't dressed to kill," Phronie muttered.

Little Dootchy was all smiles and politeness. He cut the buggy sharply, and handed his wife down with a bow that bent him half in two. Basket after basket he took from under the seat and out of the back of the buggy, all filled with delicacies he had brought up from Boston to impress the natives. There were pressed goose and duckling in jelly; elegant jars of pickled watermelon rind and spiced peach and passion fruit; tiny squat containers that held caviar and paté de foie gras; a fat red Edam cheese, and Limburger, and Brie; loaves of rye bread and pumpernickel; and huge boxes of chocolates.

"My senses," Sarah Peavy squealed, "there be enough to feed the whole kit'n caboodle on us."

Little Dootchy looked straight at Mary Jewell and smiled unpleasantly. "We don't keep any hens," he said, with what might have passed for a sneer if it hadn't sounded so polite. "So I did the best I could. In my small way."

After driving the buggy over beside the others, and unhitching his horses, he joined the men. Siah Peavy, who was the only one there to have met him, introduced him around. There were no grudges in men's minds on a day like this, and he was welcomed with the sparse words that would have been accorded any stranger.

"Well, well," he said after the round of Howdys and Pleased-to-meet-yous, "you folks don't seem to be much in the holiday mood. Now, just between us men, I've got a little something stowed away here in my wagon will put a bit of gumption inter this party. How about a bit of refreshment, gentlemen?''

Most of the men there were plain teetotalers. The hard cider they drank sparingly didn't count. A few took a sly drink of rum down in the back of Clessie Peters's store on winter evenings, and one or two of them were known to take too much now and then. But it was an unbroken tradition that, when women and children were present, lemonade was the limit.

It was Happy Tandy who broke the uncertain silence. "Why, sure enough, Mr. Duchesne. I warrant a little nip won't do no harm, 's long's the womenfolks don't git onto it.''

"Oh, this stuff won't do a thing but make you happy,'' Little Dootchy said, presenting the first bottle.

Surely, no one there, excepting perhaps John Trumbull, had ever tasted anything like it. It went down smooth as syrup, the first swallow asking sweetly for a second. By the time the ladies called them to dinner, there wasn't a really sober man among them. Chris thought it was the funniest picnic he had ever been to. He couldn't imagine what had happened to his father, who sat staring out over the pond, a jar of sturgeon's eggs in one hand and a whole duckling in the other, now and then giggling, strange conduct indeed for William Jewell. Willie Pike chattered loudly about the ways of a stallion with a mare, and Bart Jewell, in telling his Wild West stories, let out some words that even the menfolks had never heard before. Old David Mason, said to have been a great drunkard before his marriage forty years ago, just lay in the sand, kicking up his heels and guffawing. Clessie Peters found himself involved in the youngsters' game of tag, and evidenced great delight in the pursuit of Martha Benton, who was only twelve, but looked sixteen. Just as he was about to tag her, though—breast high, both hands—she sidestepped neatly and Clessie pitched forward into the pond. The water was only three inches deep, but Clessie, who couldn't swim, thought sure he would drown.

At first the womenfolks hadn't the slightest idea what was

happening. But when Siah Peavy passed up a plate of roast capon for a piece of Limburger cheese, Sarah put her finger on it without even thinking. "You must be drunk!" she said.

The incredible word was quickly whispered around.

"Drunk!"

Phronie sat paralyzed. "Wha's a matta, my little chickadee?" Bertie snickered, as he staggered up and planted a loud kiss on her cheek. "Haw, haw. Fust time I ever shut the woman's trap. Here, my own lovey dovey, gi' yer ol' man a kiss."

Phronie found her voice. "You git away from me, an' stay away, you...you...wizzled up little shrimp. I bet...I jest bet...it was that Little..." She got to her feet as she spoke.

Mary interrupted. "Sit down, Phronie, and eat your dinner. All of you. I guess if the menfolks want to take a mite of fun, it isn't going to harm anything. Do taste this delicious pickled watermelon. I guess we ladies have a lot to learn about what's good to eat. John, cut me a slice of that goose. Here, Judith, let me help you to something."

The ladies had observed Judith's face. Over her plate of food, her pale cheeks had turned to scarlet, but she sat erect and smiled. Presently, all the ladies, taking their cue from Mary Jewell, rallied around to support Judith. They stuffed themselves with food to make up for what the menfolks weren't eating. They made a point of tasting everything the Duchesnes had brought.

Phronie was loudest of all in her effort to make amends for her slip. "What on earth's this, Miz Duchesne?" she asked, peering into a jar of caviar.

"Why don't you taste it, Phronie, first, and guess," someone suggested.

Phronie managed to get a spoonful down, and the face she made was eloquent. Judith laughed aloud. "Don't try to eat any more, Mrs. Goss. It's nothing but fish eggs. Some people consider it a great delicacy, but I agree with you, it just tastes like fish eggs. It comes from Russia."

Phronie took a long sip of lemonade. "You don't say. All the way from Russia to Freckle Pond. I bet it brings a pretty penny then."

"Yes, it's rather expensive," Judith admitted.

"Waal, waal, ladies," Phronie said. "Why don't we git the boys to ketch us some horned pouts, some mother pouts, an' we c'n can up their eggs, an' ship 'em off down to Boston? I got a whole box o' them little jars Doc Gotchie keeps his hoss salve in."

Somehow or other, the day seemed to have been saved. By the time the women cleared up the mess and folded the tablecloths, the picnic ground was unnaturally quiet. Several of the men had wandered off into the woods to sleep it off.

"John," Mary said to her brother, "why don't you take Judith and me out after pond lilies? Chris!" she called to her son, who was paddling a rowboat not far from shore, "Come in and get us. We're going to pick some lilies."

Chris rowed them along the shore under the shadow of the mountain. The sweltering heat of the day had subsided. A little unaccustomed color still rested on Judith's cheekbones, but she looked lovely and collected. Only Mary could see that there was weariness in her eyes. While Chris rowed, the three of them—Judith, Mary, and John—trailed their arms in the cool water and brought up the long stems of the lilies from the muddy depths. They gathered also a few of the pads for greenery. The women were silent, but John talked at length of the lilies of the world, of great exotic blossoms resting on tropic pools, of dewy small faces bordering Alpine snows. And how the lily, like the rose, grew natively only in the northern hemisphere.

"Symbol of purity," he said, holding a dripping flower tenderly in his hand, proffering it to Judith.

She blushed as she took it. "The lilies of the field are not arrayed like one of these," she said, and thrust her face into the fragrance. "I think we must be getting back."

Little Dootchy stood spraddle-legged and belligerent on the beach as John handed Judith out of the boat. It appeared that he had not contented himself with his morning imbibing.

"Who are you?" he demanded of John.

"I am Mrs. Jewell's brother," John replied suavely. "Here are your flowers, Mrs. Duchesne."

"No man gives my wife flowers."

"She gathered the flowers for herself," John said, with all courtesy, and started to bow himself away.

"Wait a minute, you young whippersnapper. I don't stand for any liberties taken with my woman. You got out in that boat with her without my knowledge or consent. Now you're going to pay for it. By God, you are."

"I wouldn't consider this innocent pleasure an occasion for a fight, Mr. Duchesne."

Little Dootchy swayed on his spraddled legs. "I would," he said.

In the eyes of most of the bystanders, he was very drunk. That seemed to be the only explanation. Here was Little Dootchy, facing a man a good foot taller than he, and probably fifty pounds heavier, as well as ten or a dozen years younger, and demanding to fight. But Mary sensed that what she saw was in fact the real Raoul Duchesne. The malice, at any rate, was real.

"Well," John said, his voice as suave as the waters of the pond, "if you think this must be settled by fisticuffs, I suggest that we remove ourselves from the presence of the ladies."

The menfolks, sheepish-eyed and eager to make amends to their women, were not at all displeased that something had come up that bade fair to take their wives' minds off their own misbehavior. Gradually, they moved in behind Little Dootchy.

Little Dootchy appeared somewhat taken aback by John's readiness to accept his challenge. Whatever the cause, he hesitated a bit before taking a step. And when he did take one, there happened to be another foot in the way, and he went sprawling on his face. Chris thought it was Clessie Peters who had tripped him, but he couldn't be sure.

John, who knew the better part of valor, walked away, striking off toward home, crosslots and afoot. When Little Dootchy regained his feet, he found himself with not one adversary, but a dozen, each with clenched fists.

Judith stood throughout straight as a poplar tree, her cheeks touched with the color of its pallid green bark. She now handed her bouquet into Mary Jewell's hands.

"Perhaps it is time we all went home," she said. She put one hand on her husband's arm, and walked with him to their buggy.

"Well, I'll be a horse's navel," said Uncle Bart.

Sixteen

W HEN Chris came in from milking the next morning, there was a palpable pause in the conversation at the breakfast table. Uncle John was all dressed in his city clothes.

"We might as well tell him now," he said.

Mary put a plate of fritters down before her son. "Your Uncle John has a job for you boys," she said.

"I'll be wanting a couple of hired men," John explained. "I've some bookwork to do, and I shall be in Boston most of the summer, I thought perhaps you and Ed would like to make an extra cent now and then. Keep an eye on the orchard and take care of the stock. Your father says it's all right. He says Ed does enough around here to make up for what you'd do all by yourself. I figure it would be worth, say, twenty dollars a month to have my place looked after while I'm gone. Split up between you, that is."

Chris choked on his fritter. The twenty-cent bounty he got for a crow's head was the most money he'd ever seen at one time, all his own. Why, he'd be rich. His mind's eye went round and round Clessie

Peters's store, and all the things he could buy. The bargain was made.

Uncle John must have packed in the night, for Chris's first job after breakfast was to drive him down to the depot. His biggest trunk was in the back of the buckboard.

Just before they got to the village, John took his keys from his pocket and gave them into Chris's hand. And as he stepped onto the train, he put a hand on the boy's shoulder and looked him square in the eye.

"You keep an eye on things, my boy," he said solemnly. "That's all. Just keep a sharp eye."

Chris, hurrying home to help with the haying, was blown up like a pig's bladder with importance. He had stopped at Clessie's store in the village, buying a bag of chocolate creams for himself and a hood for his mother with the dollar Uncle John had advanced on his wages. But the money wasn't the most important thing. Uncle John had left him with a trust, a man-to-man trust. One thing Chris couldn't quite figure. After all, Uncle John wouldn't to gallivanting off to Boston in the summertime, leaving his garden and his cattle, for no reason at all. One thing was sure, he wasn't afraid of Little Dootchy. Chris knew his uncle better than to think that. His next thought was that Uncle John's reason had something to do with Mrs. Duchesne, not Mr. But that wasn't possible, was it?

One thing sure, he'd keep an eye out. A sharp eye.

On the morning of the fifth of July, regular as clockwork, the rite of haymaking began on William Jewell's farm. The hot suns of summer had passed their fructifying breath over the fields of timothy, the seeds of which had been brought over from England by great-great-grandfathers, and the tall ripe grass stood proud on the uplands. By the time Chris had unhitched the mare, the last drops of dew had been supped by the sun, and he took his place between his father and Uncle Bart. The long lovely rhythm of the whetted scythe began.

There was manhood in Chris that morning, and he swung his blade like a man, wide and sure, the grass falling in slanting rows like cunningly etched lines on the earth. He hardly looked up from his work all morning. Once only, he had to stop and whet his scythe, and once, when the others paused in their work to take a swig of molasses water from the jug, he tipped it up like a man and drank with satisfaction. When his mother rang the bell for dinner, he was almost abreast of his father, and was a good six paces ahead of Uncle Bart. They ate their boiled dinner and berry pie in silence, and went right back to work. All the long afternoon, Chris's short legs ached, and sweat poured down into his eyes and ran down his legs. But when they called a halt a little after four, he stood snath to snath with his father.

At supper that night, William Jewell looked at his son as though he were seeing him for the first time. "How about another helpin' o' puddin', Christopher?" he said. "Mighty good steamed puddin', Mrs. Jewell. Think we can finish that piece tomorrow, son?"

Chris flushed. He knew that, from that moment forward, his father would stop telling him, and start asking him, and that he had better have the answers ready. He hung his head in shame and pride. His father's words had fallen on him like the sword of knighthood, like the first touch of a woman, and he wanted most of all to cry. He seemed to know, all of a sudden, what growing up would mean. His mind went swiftly to Judith Duchesne.

After supper he slipped away to begin his duties for Uncle John. Judith's name had not been spoken by John when he gave his instructions, but Chris knew that she was meant among the things to be looked after. He didn't know exactly how to go about it, but he knew it was what he had to do. He saw that Little Dootchy's rig was not in the barn, and went around to the back of the house, trying to get up courage to knock and ask if there was anything he could do. He heard Big Ed wade the Brook, and was comforted to have his friend at his side. Together they could see her sitting at the kitchen table, her head on her arms.

"Criminy, she must be sick," Chris whispered, and instantly found the courage to tap loudly on the door.

She got up and came to the window. "Are you all right?" Chris timidly asked.

"Oh, it's you boys," she said, smiling. "Yes. Yes, I'm fine. I'm just fine, thank you."

"You want us to do anything...clean the hoss stalls, or something?"

"No, thank you, boys...perhaps...you'd better..."

Chris could see that one side of her face was all blue, before he saw her fall. She just crumpled up on the floor so suddenly that she was smiling at them one moment, and the next she was utterly out of sight. She might be dead for all they knew. After a second's hesitation, they rushed at the door. It was locked.

Chris cleared the stone wall in one leap on his way to get his mother. When he got back, stivvering on ahead of Mary, Big Ed had clean broken the door down, and had Judith in his arms, holding her as lightly as a child. She was just coming out of a dead faint.

"Put her down on the sofa in the sitting room," Mary ordered, "and you boys clear out of here."

"M...Mother, shall I go after Doc Sanborn?"

"Stay by, and I'll call you if we need him. Stir up the fire and put some water on to boil. Bring me a pitcher of cold water, this minute. Ed, I told you to get out of here."

But nothing on earth would have stirred Big Ed from his tracks. He just stood and passed one hand over the other while Mary unlaced stays and pulled out hairpins and bathed the bruised face with cold cistern water. It wasn't until Ed saw that Judith smiled at him that he went out of the room.

An hour passed. The boys sat on the door rock outside and chewed enough grass to fodder a cow. The Dog, lying at their feet, started up now and then, as if some memory had come into his head. He got up and trotted out to the barn. His eyes were wide open. Chris thought, if Little Dootchy had showed up then, he'd sure have a time of it getting into his own house. That Dog was just plain human.

After a time, Mary came and looked at the broken door. Ed had done a thorough job of it. It was splintered to kindling.

"Run home and get your father," Mary said to Chris, "and be quick about it."

And when William appeared, she said: "Don't ask any questions now, Mr. Jewell. Just find one of our doors that will fit this jamb, and get it hung before that man decides to come home, on a sudden."

It was midnight before the old hinges, that had been ripped away, could be restored to place, and the former door to the Jewell sink room fitted to its new place. The boys swept the scultch away and carried the splintered door over to the Jewell place. Mary looked the job over carefully, and sighed.

"It's going to show, and that's a fact. Well, that's the best we can do. I've given her some peppy tea with a little rum in it, and I guess she's sleeping now. We'd best go home."

They left Big Ed and The Dog still on the door rock from which Ed refused to budge.

So much had happened to Chris that day that he wasn't even surprised when his mother didn't send him right off to bed, but instead took down a third cup and poured him the first coffee he'd ever been allowed. He couldn't remember that he had seen his mother mad before, but she was madder than a hatter when she sat down to her coffee.

"Now, son, don't you ever repeat a word I'm saying," she began. "That man beat her, Mr. Jewell." She spoke slowly, as though to be sure that not a word would be misunderstood. There was no way to doubt the truth of what she said.

Chris could hardly believe his ears. Never in his born days had he heard of a man beating a woman. It wasn't done. His coffee went down the wrong way, and he almost choked. He kept saying, over and over again in his mind, while the silence that followed Mary's words rolled and thundered in the old kitchen, *he beat her . . . he beat her.* Sure, he knew that married folks didn't always get along. Si Elbridge had shot his wife dead, and been hanged for it, but everyone said the woman deserved it. And it was well known that old Beany Johnson and his wife, over Salisbury way, had slept in the same bed for nigh on to thirty years without speaking to each other. But no man in the recollection of the District had ever been known to beat a woman.

"And that isn't all," Mary said. "He locked all the doors and took the keys with him."

There wasn't anything else to say. Chris saw his mother break down and cry. But she didn't waste much time on that, and Chris could tell by the set of her spine when she marched into her bedroom a few minutes later, that her dander was well up and that somebody'd better watch his step.

Seventeen

MARY JEWELL slept no sleep that night. When Chris came down at four o'clock in the morning he found her in the kitchen, frying doughnuts. She put breakfast on the table and threw a shawl over her morning dress. To Chris she looked as if she'd grown inches overnight, for a good right-seeming anger always seemed to add to her stature.

"I guess she'll be up by now," she said, piling fritters on the menfolks' plates. "She's an early riser."

"Suppos'n he came home in the night?" her husband asked.

"I don't care. I'll take along some of these crullers, and 'twill look natural enough. If it wasn't for the trouble it would make for her, I'd just like to meet that man face to face. Maybe I will, one of these days."

"You want I should go?"

"No, Mr. Jewell. I'll go."

"Waal, leastwise, he can't be jealous of you."

"That shows how much you know about it, Mr. Jewell. Besides, he isn't what you'd call jealous of anyone in particular, except her. He's just jealous of her."

"Goddamn little piece of crowbait," Bart muttered. "I'm goin' to mistake him for a coyote one o' these mornin's when I'm out gunnin'."

Mary took a good long look at the kitchen door before she knocked. Her men had done a good job of it. Nobody who didn't know beforehand would know the difference. Even the old hand-wrought nails were exactly the same.

Judith came to the window when Mary tapped lightly on the door. She was dressed in a fresh morning garment, with ruching at the throat, and she had put a light dusting of powder over the dark place on her cheek. If anything, Mary thought, she looked more herself than usual. Her smile was warm and without memory, and if her eyes were tired, they had also a luster. She, too, had grown with the night, as corn grows under the lash of the storm. Mary saw that there was nothing she could do now. She felt a little foolish, hanging onto her plate of hot crullers.

"I just came over to see if you're all right," she said.

"Yes. I'm quite all right."

"I've got a key, you know, that will unlock this door. I thought perhaps you'd like it."

"It's best to leave it as it is," Judith said. "I don't want you to think I'm ungrateful..."

"Nonsense."

There was a silence. It lay heavily upon the undersong of the morning. Mary took the bull by his horns: "You aren't going to let him keep you locked up in this house, be you, Judith Duchesne?"

"I have never thought of any other way, Mary," Judith said, "to keep peace in my house. He bought this place, this house, because he thought no one could get at me here. He knew all about the house when he bought it. He'll be back today sometime, with locks that cannot be fitted with ordinary keys. I'm surprised he hasn't done it before. He thought you folks, you Yankee people, were an unfriendly lot, and wouldn't..."

"Judith Duchesne," Mary said, her voice carved out of hard-grained wood, "never in my whole life has it once occurred to me to ask a woman to leave her husband. But if you will get together a few things now, and come over to our house, we'll see to it that he can't get at you.

There's plenty in this District would be glad to give him whatfor, just on principle. The word 'divorce' has never passed my lips before, but it's passing them now."

"My husband is a Catholic, you know, Mary. There's nothing more I can say."

"But . . . but *locked* in your own house! . . . Why, child, it's plain unthinkable. *Unthinkable!*"

"It isn't the first time, Mary." For a moment her eyes went a little frantic. "I . . . I have much to do to keep my house in order. My husband is a model of devotion . . . just as long as . . . as nobody . . . *nobody* . . ."

"Yes. I know. Even me, Judith."

"Even you. I shall . . . miss you . . . you know . . . But . . ."

"Don't worry, my child. I'll be right here, if anything happens. Anytime, remember . . . night or day . . ."

Mary went slowly home, still carrying the plate of crullers. At noontime, she was still as if in a trance.

As she served her husband his meal, he asked, "How'd you make out, Mrs. Jewell?"

"I didn't make out, Mr. Jewell."

"Waal, did you make in?"

"No . . . no. And no one else, either. Poor child . . . poor child. I can't think what . . . what to do . . . what to do."

The four of them ate their dinner in silence, each of them thinking of what to do, what to do, and each of them coming to a blind end.

In spite of one of her rare sick headaches, Mary sat down that afternoon and wrote to her brother.

Mary, my dear [he replied], the world of men is a jungle world still, and love a jungle passion, and women put their heads upon the block of it. I am minded to go abroad this summer, for I do not see how otherwise I can endure to stay away. I must put distance and time between her and my thoughts of her. I have just now learned of a woman over in Amherst who has for thirty years shut herself away from the world altogether, for a tragedy of love. She is writing poetry. All we can hope now for Judith is either some miraculous release, or that she will make of her life, as Emily Dickinson has done, a song. I have been privileged to see some of Miss Dickinson's verses, as I have a friend who visits her occasionally, and wish I could somehow convey them to Judith, along with her sad story. But even this I cannot do, I know. She will not diminish with her sorrow. Perhaps the child will make a difference to him, but that I doubt. His case is not so rare as you might think. I have known men who kept all sorts of rare possessions out of the sight of any other eyes but their own. They are the misers of this world, and never learn that, by trying to possess, they lose life itself, and most of all destroy the very things they cherish. But she will not be destroyed, and if you wish to help her, as I know you do, as I do; all we can give her now is prayer and patience and hope. Tell the boy to try to keep Ed away. Much as we'd like to think it is, good is not always a match for evil in this world, and innocence is a fragile flower, even when it grows on a mighty stalk. And for my sake, keep a vigil yourself.

The Jewell family agreed never to speak a word to outsiders of Judith Duchesne's incarceration. But there was little hope it wouldn't somehow leak out, and it was only a day or two afterward that Siah Peavy, finding a swarm of bees, remembered that he had lent his bee bonnet to Bertie Huggins the summer before, and he went over to the Duchesnes' to get it back. Bertie hadn't thought to return it, but he wasn't the sort to have taken it back to Portsmouth with him either. Siah might have to look for it himself, but he was pretty sure it would be there.

Siah was in a great hurry to hive the bees before they took off for parts unknown. Judith was shaking rugs out of an upper window when he ran into the back yard and called up to her.

"Why, yes," she said, without having to think about it, "there's a bee bonnet on the top shelf of the buttery."

"Waal, don't you bother to come down, Miz Duchesne. I'll just pop in and get it, if you don't mind. Those dod-ratted bees'll be off . . ." He had put his hand to the latch of the kitchen door. "God bless me, it's locked," he called up to her.

After supper that evening, the Peavys visited the Jewells. "What's goin' on over to the Duchesne place?" Siah wanted to know. "That woman was locked into her house this mornin'. Had to fetch that bee bonnet clean upstairs an' throw it outen the window to me. Said she guessed her husband had went off and fergot to leave the keys."

Mary said, rather lamely, "Well, I suppose he must have, then."

"Now, Mary Jewell, you're coverin' somethin' up, I c'n tell by the set o' yer mouth," Sarah said. "An' besides, Siah says the lock on the kitchen door was shinin' new, the kind you haff to git a special key for."

"Like as not, he's 'fraid she'll git scared by tramps when he's off away," William put in.

"Humph," Sarah grunted.

That was quite enough. Sarah ran over and told Phronie the next morning, and they decided to make a call on Judith Duchesne. Little Dootchy had returned, so they bided their time till he should leave again. As they came up the walk the day they knew the coast was clear, they saw Judith through the open door of the pantry, moving about in the kitchen, but when they knocked, they got no response. Phronie banged the great iron knocker a second time. Still, no answer. Then, quietly, she tried the door handle.

"Mercy on us, Sarah," she said in a loud voice, "I hope she ain't sick. We'd better go round the back way."

Getting no answer there either, the two of them went straight to the Jewell house. Phronie was in high dudgeon.

"Now don't you try to tell me, Mary Jewell," she said, "that that woman ain't locked up in that house, for sure. She don't answer the back or front door, she don't, an' we seed her there, right in the house. You jest plain ain't goin' to make me believe she don't want us there. An' I bin watchin' her house a week come tomorrer, an' she don't even put out her wash, 'ceptin' he's home. So there."

"We haven't any right, Phronie, to interfere with other folks' lives," was all the answer Mary would make.

It sufficed. Word was all over Schoodac District before sundown that Little Dootchy kept his wife prisoner in her own house. And it was not rumor. Mary Jewell herself had confirmed it.

Eighteen

ONE day the next week, Ed's father cut himself badly with the scythe. Ed, coming home in the early evening from one of his long treks over Kearsarge way, saw The Dog prick up his ears and sniff, and thought there must be a hedgehog after nubbins in one of the apple trees. He followed The Dog through the hayfield and found his father where he had been lying all afternoon in the glaring sun, blood all over him.

The nearest house was the Jewells'. Ed came bursting into the kitchen. "It be m' paw, Miz Jewell. He be all blood . . . all over blood."

Mary called her menfolks and rushed out to see what she could do. Ed and Bart carried Mr. Cheney into his own house, while Chris drove as fast as he could to fetch Doc Sanborn. Mr. Cheney refused to be taken to the Jewell house.

"The boy'll take care of me," he said. "That's one thing he's good at. Took every mite o' the care o' his Aunt Fanny before she died. Waited on her hand and foot."

"But you'll need food, good nourishing food," Mary argued. "You've lost a lot of blood."

"We eat simple here, ma'am. We'll manage. Reckon I'm jest plain used to my own bed 'n' board. Thankin' ye, jest the same."

Doc Sanborn said Mr. Cheney wouldn't be cutting any more hay for quite a spell. Come Sunday, the neighbors got together and cut his timothy, with Big Ed tramping down the loads, and Chris raking after.

Ed was as good as his father's word. Mary, expecting the house of a couple of batching men to be all cluttered up, if not filthy, found it almost nasty neat. The Jewell family meanwhile settled down without a riffle to care for three farms. Nobody gave a thought to the extra burden. The working day was simply extended a few hours. By four in the morning, everyone was up and at it, and the evening chores were done by lantern light. It wasn't the way of a New Hampshireman to boggle at a little work. When Mary made pies or baked biscuits, an extra pan went into the oven. Chris milked his father's cows first, then Uncle John's, and thence on to the two Jerseys at the Cheney place. Big Ed had tried and tried, but he just couldn't milk a cow. His hands were too big.

It had been Mr. Cheney's custom to drive down to the village on Saturday afternoons for his week's provender. A methodical man, he never varied a habit, and so it was that Big Ed began making a weekly appearance at The Corners.

At first, he and The Dog caused quite a little stir. Folks stared at them, and crossed the street to avoid The Dog. But they soon found that, under Ed's smoothing words, the great beast was as meek as Moses. They began to answer Ed's unfailing grin, and to take no little pride in the very monstrosity of the pair. They were pointed out to summer visitors, and whispered about as smugly as if they were something newly captured from the jungle and unique to this one community. Like everyone else in the world, the villagers liked being just a little frightened of something.

From the moment Ed's wheaten thatch came over the rise at the head of Maple Street, the main thoroughfare, a titivation of interest would run through the customers at Clessie Peters's store. Ed would come up the three steps that led from the boardwalk, grinning all across his face. He never bothered to hitch up the rig. There wasn't much on his list anyway. Once he had the weekly farm journal from Happy Tandy, he went into Clessie's. Into his vast pockets would go a sack of coffee beans, a hank of wool—for Mr. Cheney knitted his own socks—a tin of bag balm, a packet of whole cloves.

Ed had no more sense about money than a squirrel, and Mary had written her brother when the first twenty dollars had come in, to ask if he didn't think it wise to hold out most of Ed's share against the day when he would have to look out for himself. John had replied firmly:

"Let the boy have his money to spend. Perhaps it's best to give it him in weekly installments. Don't worry about Ed. I'll set aside a portion for him. But if I'm right about the boy, Mary, he might as well spend it while he can."

So, after Ed had passed his father's list to Clessie, he'd poke about the store, buying the most outrageous things, the things he took a fancy to. He had observed that Judith Duchesne always wore a bit of lace at throat and wrist, so he bought whole cards of cheap lace to give to her. He bought her a pair of fancy gloves, and once he bought her a hat, much to the amusement of everyone. Clessie helped him pick things out, not because Clessie wanted Ed's money, but because Clessie was a kind man, and he'd taken a fancy to Ed and The Dog.

His purchases all stowed about his person, Ed would find himself at the candy counter, and Clessie would fill him up a brown paper sack with chocolate creams and nougats and peppermint sticks.

The second time Ed visited the store, Clessie called him back as he started to leave.

"Reckon you forgot somethin', Ed," he said. "Hold on a minute."

He made a quick move into the room where he hung his meat, and returned with a huge, well-meated bone. "That feller goin' to bite me, if I give him this?"

"He don't bite, Mister Peters, 'ceptin' he has to. Look, Dod. Take it nice, now."

And off they went, up Maple Street, with people gawking at them. And no wonder. Ed bulged all over with his purchases. Over one shoulder he had slung a sack of meal, and under the other arm he carried a whole ham. From his mouth stood the stick of candy he was sucking, and a bright red ribbon flowered from one pocket. Beside him walked The Dog, holding aloft his bone. No Saturday was complete without this little show.

People still kept a respectful distance from The Dog, especially after the day he tipped over a barrel of potatoes upon seeing Quint Haley step across the threshold. But they marveled more at Ed's quiet governance of his pet than they did at the thought that anything or anyone should take umbrage at Quint Haley. Clessie entertained them with the story of the schoolhouse incident until they all clucked in admiration, and unanimously declared The Dog to be more than half human.

"I swan," said Happy Tandy, watching the two of them go up the street, "I don't hanker ter aggravate that crittur. But I'd give my bottom dollar to own him. I know a coupla folks I'd like to sic him onto."

Nineteen

THE great earth waits for no man. Over meadow and cornfield and pasture walked July, tossing her tassled head, throwing about her ample shoulders and feather boa of posy bed and hardhack bloom and purple sumac head, hussying after August. On the checkered tablecloths of Schoodac District, the sweet corn piled in pyramids, and the first earth-fragrant tomatoes ran their juices on bearded chins. Shaded beside rill and run, the ripened blackberries hid coyly beneath leaf and thorn, and daintily the muskmelons tasted their own golden sweetness under the hum of bumblebees. Across the northern sky at evening, the aurora borealis waved peacock-feather fans, foretelling the hot dawn, and haycock and stubble field proclaimed the zenith of the year, wrought into the hard coin of next winter's foddering. The singing of breadfruit was heard in all the land.

Through it all they waited, the folks along the Brook. Siah Peavy, building a new pen for his shoats, thought of the woman he might have married, had he had the luck, a woman tall enough to hold his dreams. He dreamed of riding to her window some dark night on a white charger, and fetching her afar from Sarah's pinched face. Bart Jewell tried hard to think up words to take the place of one half of his vocabulary, and only arrived at more and better cussing. Mary Jewell, bent over her hot stove canning beans, sighed so much that William said her coffin was already so nailed down she'd never have a chance to get into it. Even Phronie Goss, singing the first eight bars of "Onward, Christian Soldiers" to time her breakfast eggs, forgot to snatch a swatch of Bertie's hide with her tongue every time she set eyes on him.

Mary had promptly written to her brother concerning the beating and the boys' discovery of it. John's reply came from a fishing village on the coast of Norway.

MY DEAR SISTER MARY,

I am urgent with the need to be with you; with her. And so, as ever, I take my refuge in my Plato, trying to learn that this brief love of one beautiful form must lead me to the knowledge and the contemplation of all beauty, forswearing the one. To learn to be a non-lover, and so a lover of beauty itself. Alas, I have but small success of such great endeavor! I thought to be a Socrates, and "only hold a book before my nose," but the words dissolve to dreaming and desire, and I am but a man like other men, torn in two by the wish to throttle another man and the passion to take his wife. The finest sentiments about the paradox of being in love, its fleetingness and "ample guerdon" bestowed and then turned cold, but find me gazing out my window at the tall lovely spruces here, that so much resemble Judith, their lordly heads held high, their back hair streaming in the wind.

This is my confession, and I need not have made it to you, who knew it all along. Hourly, I hold to my leash, and every small fishing boat I see ploughing the waves westward stretches the chain almost to the breaking point. I know I must, in plain duty to her, keep this distance, and try to remember that it is not so great, in truth, as it would be were I sitting in my library at Schoodac while these unspeakable atrocities take place, and I more than helpless, either to avert or succor.

I know her well, as I have known men like him. And what I read of history and of life teaches me patience. I think of her, in calmer moments, as growing old, marvellously; of making of her imprisonment a tower of such transcendent joy that one day he will fall a prisoner, too, and all the things that now torment her spirit will be transmuted into a holy indifference that is the absolute of love.

Jealousy, like virtue, is its own reward, and he cannot but reap his whirlwind. Sometimes at night I can a little console myself that the day will come, if now a long time off, when we shall all once more sit by your hearth, and I can read to her all the beautiful passages in the books that I have marked down for her hearing.

Praise God, we all believe in miracles, and live by this belief. To fall in love with one's own unrequited love has been the portion of better men than I, and is more often than we know the lot of womankind.

As for Ed, there is nothing anyone can do. If I am not entirely wrong in my reading of his case, his span will not be long in any event. He has not the capacity to love as other men love. Of this I feel quite sure. His happinesses and his despairs are those of a child, brief and terrible, and his devotion pure. I know your careful love will shield him as it may and while it can. If there is anything of mine he takes a liking to, the mare, the Jersey cow, a rat in the grain bin, give it him. It will not abate his obsession, for his obsession is a sheltering mother love. But it will take up his time, and that is the most any of us can ever hope to have, something to take our time from birth to death.

I am writing Chris to comfort him from thinking he has

broken his trust. I know him well enough to know better. I know he is losing the sleep of boyhood in my cause. But perhaps we are giving him something he will remember, and a sense of responsibility he will carry on through life. His own devotion to her will remain in his memory for the instruction of the woman he will some day marry, long after the sordid events of today have lost their power over him, and will direct him rather toward loving than toward horsewhipping.

I suppose I have, like any other lover, written this letter in the vain hope that she will see it. Keep it among your things, if you will, against the day when she may be comforted to know that she is loved. I cannot even dream that she, with her implacable integrity, would judge it anything but unthinkable that a married woman would give second thoughts to another man, or that, even in other circumstances, she would be so gracious as to choose me from the world of men who would be at her feet, were she free. But it is good to know that one is loved, and I have not the sort of pride to make me hesitate to tell her so. I shall never love another woman, of that I am as certain as the day, were the day infinity.

No, there is naught that you can do for me, except to reach her if and when you can, to give her the wholesomeness—the holiness—of your understanding love. Keep me posted about her, and send me a cablegram the very moment... but wait, I won't finish that. Old Hope has sprung up again, that hydra-headed slave at love's feast. My parting words to you and to her come from our great, martyred President: 'Trusting in Him who can go with me and remain with you.'

Forever,

JOHN

Post Script. Will you be so very kind as to send me the marker in my Bible, the blue ribbon that Great-Aunt Patience stitched for me: "Umquil in Plesure and Prosperitie; Umquil in Pane and greit Penuritie."

Twenty

CLESSIE PETERS sat lackadaisically spatting flies on a bin of overripe bananas. The morning was sultry and silent. Only the whistle of the milk train as it left Joppa on its way down to The Corners, and the various clop-clops of horses carrying cream to the depot cleft the heavy air. Clessie could tell each horse without going to the window by now: George Goodwin's high-stepping filly, dancing a few extra paces now and then; Dave Mason's old clodhopper, treading his heavy two-step, stopping, staring back at Dave's urgent, shrill cry, "Git up, Susie...git up, thar"; William Jewell's young gelding, with Chris at the reins; Daniel Hardy's pacer. The train rumbled over the trestle and ground to a stop. In a few minutes would come the usual morning trade: a half pint of gin, a gallon of molasses, a length of diaper cloth. It's high time Annie Flint was buying diapers again, Clessie thought. He was trying to figure out why she always got it in seven-yard pieces when he heard outside the unmistakable hooving of the Duchesne bays. Little Dootchy came swaggering in.

"Mornin', Mr. Dootchane," Clessie said grudgingly.

Little Dootchy was in no mood to talk. He placed a twenty-dollar gold piece on the counter, and the sun, just coming over Doc Sanborn's house, seemed to grab it, polishing to a bright glitter.

"For that whip," he said. Little Dootchy nodded in the direction of a long horsewhip stretched out on a series of pegs behind the counter, the place of honor.

Clessie picked up his fly spatter, and spatted at nothing at all. He knew that Little Dootchy knew the story of that whip. He wondered what the man was up to.

"Dunno's I ever cal'lated ter part with that p'tikler whup," he said.

"Didn't think you did, Mr. Peters. But Christ, man, there's a price on everything. How much? How much?"

"Ain't sellin'."

Clessie looked uncomfortably at the twenty-dollar gold piece. Only that morning, Prudence had been nagging him again about a new bonnet and shawl, about his softheartedness. The whip had been hanging there a long time now, gathering dust and fly specks. Hardly anyone noticed it anymore. Once in a great while, a new drummer would be sitting around swapping yarns of a winter night, and someone would tell him the story of Deacon Plummer and his bull.

Clessie couldn't quite get his argument straight in his mind. The whip was his, to do what he wanted to with. But it was a sort of town property, too; it belonged by unwritten rights to every manjack in all the surrounding country. It was more than a horsewhip. It was a symbol. Men laughed a little and pushed their hands deeper into their pockets whenever they thought of it, letting out a gusset in their pride.

Deacon Plummer had been cold in his grave this ten years now, but he was still hot in memory. Little Dootchy, now that Clessie thought of it, reminded him of the Deacon. They made a pair, them two, and there would be something downright traitorous in letting the mean little Canuck have the whip. They were both slickers. The Deacon had been built a good deal like Little Dootchy, short and swaggery and always fidgeting about something. The Deacon took the same kind of pride in his bull that Little Dootchy took in his pair of bays. No, Clessie corrected himself, the same kind Little Dootchy took in his wife. The difference was not very great, perhaps.

The Deacon had had a sulphur-and-molasses way about him, just like Raoul Duchesne. He wasn't so bad to the taste until you knew the purpose of him. When you knew it was going to run you off at the bowels, it didn't taste so good. Sundays, all dressed up in a swallowtail coat and a collar that practically tipped him over backward, the Deacon had passed the plate at the Congregational Church and praised the Lord in the front row of the choir. He always managed to get himself appointed as a pallbearer when the village's most prominent citizens died, and carried himself with a comical dignity, his corner of the coffin sloping off to'ds Sawyer's, as the villagers liked to say. No one ever forgot the day he let go and fell into the grave just as the minister was about to intone the dust-to-dust. But even then, he had dusted himself off and foreclosed the mortgage on the deceased's farm before the widow got home from the burying. If a neighbor got into a tight spot, especially a widow woman, Deac was always on hand to offer a measly price in his mealy voice for a horse or a cow, buttering up the deal by throwing in a bushel of windfalls or a cracked whiffletree.

The Deacon hadn't been able to keep his paws off a stray cow. No one had ever been able to prove a thing against him, but one or two had sneaked into his hovel at night and found missing property there. More commonly, a cow would have been sold at some auction a piece upstate before it was even missed.

Deacon Plummer had one possession he prized above anything, a fine handsome holstein bull he'd brought home as a calf and raised himself. Some said the Deacon wouldn't pay the price of keeping a wife, and kept the bull instead. His neighbors, always desirous of improving their stock, had no other choice but the scrub bulls thereabouts. They swore lustily at the cost of standing him, but they took their cows to him. Deac took their money first, and afterward, in the only moments of personal expansiveness he ever showed, brought out a pitcher of good hard cider. Toasts were drunk, mostly addressed to the bull, until the Deacon was tipsy.

People said the bull despised the Deacon as much as they did, that only a good supply of heifers propitiated his wrath. And one day the bull turned on his master and gored him. One horn went right up his rectum, Clessie's father, passing by at that moment, had said. The bull held him up in the air for a moment, then tossed his head and Deac flew across the barnyard.

He managed to crawl under the fence, calling on Almighty God in words taken straight out of the Good Book, but somewhat misapplied in their context. Mr. Peters rushed for Doc Sanborn, and the Deacon, his lower bowels hanging out of his pants, managed to get as far as the hallway of his house, prop his gun on a barrel of apples, and shoot the crittur dead. Clessie's father and the Doc found the two of them in their blood, and Mr. Peters had gone out and cut off the bull's penis, from which the whip was made.

It was an exact sort of justice, the kind men understood. That, and the manner of his demise.

"That ol' son of a sea cook," drawled Happy Tandy in his precise way of speaking, "always did transact his business straight outen his backsides."

Clessie eyed Little Dootchy narrowly. "They's other whups. Just as good."

Little Dootchy put down another gold coin. By this time, Happy Tandy had distributed the mail from upstate, and menfolks had gathered in the store for their morning exchange of comments on crops and weather. Silently, incredulously, they stood staring at the two spots of gold on the counter, as if they would dissolve in the sunshine at any moment, leaving only the alloy of their disdain for Little Dootchy.

Clessie scratched the back of his neck and looked around him for help. He said many times afterward that he couldn't have been thinking of anything at all but the sum of forty dollars. Times, he didn't make much more than that in a month's hard work. Likely, there wasn't a man there who wasn't thinking the same thing. In the ordinary run of affairs, men of New Hampshire gathered like an oak burl over the problems common to them all, and there was no man there who wouldn't have been glad to chip in money to match Little Dootchy's, or at least to have given him a run for it. But this was no ordinary matter, and they stood shifting uneasily in their boots.

Someone spoke up at last, a bit uncertainly. "Pick it up, Clessie. Pick it up."

Clessie picked it up.

"Help yourself," he said shortly.

"Take it down," Little Dootchy ordered, but Clessie had already stepped into the back room. The others stood and watched while Little

Dootchy climbed up on a cracker barrel and took down his whip.

The group moved as a body to the front window to see him untie his horses from the hitching rail and go off down the street.

"It ain't no matter, Clessie," someone called when he was out of sight. "We'd all a' done the same thing. Whew, forty dollars, by God."

"What in thunderation he wants it fer, that bad, that's what beats me," Clessie said, returning to the front room. "I ain't never see him lay a whip ter them fancy nags o' his'n. By God, I feel downright ashamed o' myself, givin' in ter that little shit like that."

"Aw, jest a god-wallopin' show-off, that's all."

"Prob'ly aimin' ter use it on the old woman," Hank Peabody from up Burnhap way suggested.

Chris Jewell, who had come in to get a spool of thread for his mother, was stunned by the words, remembering the sound of a whip he had heard in the night. Clessie opened his mouth with an oath: "By the living Jehoshaphat, if I thought for a minute..."

And suddenly it was as if the whip itself had stung every man there to the quick. As if the symbol had come to life again. Helpless, the men forgot their errands and hurried home to tell their wives. Chris, on his way home, saw Siah Peavy, fifty yards ahead, take his wagon whip out of its socket to lash his old mare up Butter Hill, and suddenly stand up straight in his buckboard and throw the whip as far as he could hurl it, over the wall by the road.

By dinner time, the whole countryside was buzzing like a swarm of hornets.

Twenty-one

O n a late afternoon when the red raspberries had ripened in the newly timbered-off lot up back of Uncle John's, Chris and Big Ed took their buckets over their arms and went off to gather the fruit. There were a good many thunderstorms that July, but then, July was always brewing up something in the way of a downpour. Thunder had rumbled around the horizon all day, and Chris had tramped down seven loads of meadow hay, with Ed tossing up huge forksful to him. Ed seemed to catch the electricity from the air, and it excited him to a kind of fury. This particular afternoon he seemed as happy as of old, loping along ahead of Chris, rattling the tin measuring cup into which the berries were to be picked before being dumped in the bucket, grinning at the antics of The Dog and the steer, both of which followed.

The timber lot stood at the edge of a swamp on the farther side of the Brook, and the raspberries were fat thimbles of claret beauty under the cover of their leaves. Chris and Ed lay on their backs on a great boulder, the fruit that overhung them within easy reach and ripe for plucking. Chris knew that part of Ed's excitement was for the storm that was passing safely around them, and part of it the gathering of an offering for Judith Duchesne. He was a little worried, for there wasn't much he could do with Ed in this mood. Little Dootchy hadn't been home for almost a week, and must be about due. Chris would sure have to keep a sharp eye tonight. Once or twice, already, he had averted possible trouble by waiting for Little Dootchy to start snoring, and then sneaking over to retrieve some gift or other of Ed's. But today, his quick senses alive to every mood and tense of what went on about him, he felt a hollow feeling in the pit of his stomach. If it didn't turn to rain, the moon would be up, and anything might happen.

They were stripping the bushes within reach of the last berries when they heard a thin little cry. The Dog sat up and quivered, and Ed, spilling his bucket of berries as he clambered to his feet, spoke to him to stop his whining. Chris put his almost-full bucket in a safe place, under a tall pine that had been saved for seedling, and together they stood for a moment to locate the direction of the cry. Weakly and more weakly it came, as they followed it. Every now and then they had to stop for long minutes at a time before it sounded. Even The Dog, who had no scent to go by, got them off in the wrong direction. The clutter of branch and limb and standing stump that had been left by the woodsmen stayed their progress, and every now and then the steer refused to budge, and Big Ed had to pick him up and carry him a piece.

The long shadow of Kearsarge had fallen athwart the horizon eastward before they at last discovered it. They saw the white flag of the mother as she turned tail and fled uphill. The Dog got the fawn by the throat before Big Ed saw its unblinking, fear-stricken eyes between two fallen logs. It was mired in the bog to its knees and its mouth was panting open from its struggle. Big Ed called The Dog off and wallowed in, heaving the logs apart, and slowly, tenderly, coaxingly, working the little creature free. It was far spent with weariness and hunger, and on its throat were the marks of The Dog's canines. But it was breathing. It trembled all over when Big Ed picked it up.

Chris said, "If you put it down, there on the edge of the solid ground, its mother'll come back after it. It isn't true they don't come back."

But he knew when he said it, it was no use. Ed just stood there, his feet in a puddle, and crooned and cried with joy. His big face fairly shone in the darkening of the day. One huge hand cupped the speckled butt, and the other ran up and down flank and backbone until the creature stopped trembling and accepted the cradle of Big Ed's arms, laying its soft head against his shoulder like a baby.

Chris had a tussle getting home. He carried his bucket of berries in one hand, and Ed's empty pail in the other, and every now and then he was forced to set them down and round up the calf, who had no mind to go any farther that day. He was excited, himself. No other boy that he knew had ever had a deer for a pet. Quite a cavalcade they would make now, with Dog and steer and doe tagging after. They'd bed her down in Ed's woodshed on a pile of straw. The Dog would soon enough get used to her.

He didn't think of anything else all the way home, except how late he'd be with his chores. When they got there, they found that his father was off down at The Corners at a meeting of the selectmen, and that Uncle Bart had done the milking. Chris dashed up attic where he remembered seeing a cache of nursing bottles, and, with his mother's help, the boys got a little warm milk down the fawn's throat. Mary Jewell wanted them to bed it down back of the kitchen stove, where nothing could get at her for the night, but Big Ed refused to leave her. His eyes still held that holy joy, and he babbled to her a sort of lullaby, like the ineffably tender gurglings of a crow to her nestlings.

Ed put her down on an old quilt beside his father's bed while he fixed supper for him and while Chris milked his cows. While milking, Chris remembered that he hadn't shut up his chickens, so he ran back home as soon as he finished.

By the time he'd eaten the supper his mother set out for him, night had fallen, a hot sultry night with sheet lightning and fireflies lying on the air in waves of listlessness. Chris was tired and sweaty and decided to take a swim before going to bed. When he got to the Brook he saw that the slab-faced moon had tumbled like a one-sided Red Astrakhan over the hill. He didn't think much about it, and was floating deadman in the swimming hole when he saw Big Ed come down the field with the fawn in his arms, going straight for the Duchesne place. It suddenly came to Chris what all Ed's joy had been about: he had found the perfect gift for his lady.

Chris's mind went into a whirlpool. He knew Little Dootchy was at home. He'd come home late last night. Chris cursed himself for neglecting his trust. This was the first night since Uncle John had gone away, leaving her to his care, that he hadn't hovered about her house until her light went out. . . . And after Little Dootchy had bought the whip, he'd sat scrunched up on the end of the ledge every night, waiting for the crack of that whip. He had it all planned out, that if he ever heard that sound, he'd run for his father, who would somehow take the matter into his own hands. Father and Doc Sanborn were judge and jury and justice itself in the District, and there were many dark things they settled between them. The whole complicated problem had got almost too much for a boy, what with remembering Sabina's words, and thinking all the time how to keep vigil on Judith Duchesne. It was a lot to expect of a boy to get it all straight in his mind, and he had just about forgotten Big Ed's part in it. He was so used to keeping Ed away from Little Dootchy that he'd lost track of the reasons for it, and now, when he did think of them, they seemed unimportant beside the problem of keeping her from harm.

But that suddenly changed. It came to him, seeing Bid Ed come down through the cornfield toward her house, that just in this way could she be most hurt. He understood, as well as a boy might, Little Dootchy's jealousy of Uncle John. But that he should be jealous of Big Ed had not occurred to Chris, and he would have thought it ridiculous if it had. He put down Little Dootchy's behavior toward Ed as anger at being kept awake at night. After all, Ed's devotion to the lady next door was comparable indeed to Chris's own.

He paddled to shore and met Ed before he crossed. "You come on home with me," Chris said, but could see that he might as well have been in Timbuctoo for all Ed heard.

Without pausing, Ed splashed across the Brook. Chris glued to his tracks and naked, saw a light come on in the upper window, saw the tail of Little Dootchy's nightshirt disappear through the door, heard the clatter of slippers on the stairs.

Ed stood under the window, a few feet from the door rock. He held the fawn aloft, and he chanted, "I dot a deer for you. I dot a little deer . . . a tiny little deer. . . ."

The kitchen door flew on its hinges, and Little Dootchy stood there, holding something in his hand.

Ed took no notice. Suppliant at his altar, he continued singing his perfect song.

The whip cut a black spiral in the air. The Dog, leaping twice his length, sank his teeth into the hand that held it.

Chris realized at that moment that Little Dootchy had never seen The Dog before.

"Dod!" Ed cried. "Dod!"

The Dog let go.

Little Dootchy got himself behind the kitchen door in the shake of a lamb's tail, and the things he was saying were as ugly as the snarl in The Dog's throat.

Big Ed came slowly back across the Brook. When he passed Chris, his face was drawn down in terrible grief. He made no sound, but his whole great body seemed to shrink away in one deafening unvoiced threnody. The head of the fawn hung loose against his shoulder, its lolling tongue a black blot on all light.

Chris lay a long time on the bank of the Brook that night. The tears he would have liked to shed had dried up within him, the tears that but lately had been a boy's. He heard Big Ed, stumbling, pass between the cornstalks. He saw the moon draw about herself a dark hood of cloud. The sweat turned cold along his loins, and the despair of manhood was a rock and an anchor within him.

He heard Little Dootchy scream to his wife, and saw her put a white robe over her nightclothes and go down to the kitchen. She poked up the fire, boiled water, and fetched a bottle of liniment from a cupboard. Quietly she bathed and bound the injured hand, her husband whimpering like a baby when he wasn't cursing like a sailor. She disappeared from Chris's sight for a moment, and came back bearing a decanter.

When they got back to the upstairs chamber, Chris heard him scream: "The minute I can use this damned hand, I'll lick the daylights out of you...you Jezebel...you hot cheap ruttin slut...you *bitch!*"

Judith Duchesne stood facing him like a statue of white ice, only her hair seeming alive, and he struck her on the face with his good hand.

"Now come to bed...with *me*," he shouted.

After waiting what seemed an unmeasurable time, Chris heard Little Dootchy begin to snore. Getting to his feet, catlike, Chris made a long detour around by fields to avoid the sound of his feet in the water, crept up to the Duchesne house and got the whip. When he went down with the cream the next morning, he took the whip back to Clessie and told the congregation of menfolks the whole story. He just couldn't keep it in. It was only fair that they should know.

Clessie got out some long staples and fixed the whip back in its place. No one had spoken a word at Chris's telling. But Clessie gave him a bag of chocolates, and Chris could see by the faces of the others that they had taken the problem of Little Dootchy out of his hands.

But he had plenty of time on his way home to regret his action. His father would hear of it, surely, and Chris would probably get the horsewhipping of his life. As he unhitched the gelding, he decided it would be better to confess and have it over with.

The words tumbled out of him while he left his breakfast untouched. Out of the corner of his eye he watched his father's face, saw him lay his two-tined fork beside his plate, and saw a dreaded look come into his eye.

"I guess I . . . I shouldn't of done it," he said miserably.

"Waal, boy, I dunno," his father said. "Ef you'd ha' come to me, like you planned, thar warn't nothin' I could o' done. Not then and there. Thar be a time for keepin' yer mouth shut. But thar be a time for openin' it, too. Folks is noisy enough ter prate o' things that be'nt their business. But I callalate this here thing's got to the place where it's the business o' every decent manjack in these parts. You keep your eyes open an' tell me everything you see. Times us menfolks got to stick together."

"The goddamn dirty little bastard," Uncle Bart put in. "I got a rope. Just a teeny twist o' the wrist, an' . . ."

"Bart," Mary admonished, but the word had a ring of relief in it.

Twenty-two

ENCOURAGED a little, Chris wolfed down his breakfast. As soon as he was done, he hustled off to the Cheneys' to milk their cows. Big Ed was not there.

His father, hobbling painfully about the house, was creased with worry. "I'm damned if I know what got into the boy," he said. "He took the death o' that deer *that* hard! Warn't like himself at all this mornin'. Dug a grave out there under the pearmain tree. Ye can see it from here. Like to spaded up the whole orchard, he did. Threw up dirt everywhere. I ain't never seed him mad before, not downright mad. Got himself down in that hole side o' the crittur. I didn't think s' much o' that. Had a time buryin' his Aunt Fanny, he was that determint to git in beside her. I ain't never worrit when Ed bawls. But ne'er a sound outen him this day. Jest thunder looks an' throwin' things. Same thing with The Dog. Growled all the mornin'. I was plumb scairt o' him. Waal, they's off somewheres."

Chris told him what happened last night, adding a word about Little Dootchy's cast of mind.

"Ayah, I knowed. 'Tain't much I c'n do about it, my dodratted ol' leg like this, an' gettin' wuss, seems like."

"You'd better stay off it, Mr. Cheney," Chris said. "I'll see to the chores, an' we'll pick your early apples soon's they're ready."

"Mighty good neighbors, you folks. No, it's the boy I'm fretted of. His ma's folks was all a mite off in the head. Jest a mite. Had an uncle, quiet's a mouse. But times he'd git som'at in him an' throw the wagon right across the road. I jest don't know what this throwin' business'll come to, that's all."

Dutiful Ed came home in time to get his father's evening mush and milk. He came with his arms full of flowers, and Chris, there for the evening milking, thought he'd probably go and dump them all on Judith Duchesne's doorstep, and he, Chris, would have to wait up and take care of that somehow. He had seen Little Dootchy setting off at dawn, his right arm in a sling under his coat. The buggy turned onto the road to Concord, so Little Dootchy wasn't going to see Doc Sanborn, as anyone else would have done. That was like the man, Chris thought.

But Ed didn't take the flowers to Judith. He silently gathered up a dozen or so jars and pots, and put them all on the fawn's grave. Hardhack in rosy spikes, primrose and milkweed pod, and the first blooms of goldenrod. Big Ed's morning mood had so completely left him that he seemed emptied of everything. His face was drawn and peaked; even sorrow had no place on it.

Chris couldn't get a word out of him, so he went down alone for his evening swim. He was lying naked on the ledge when he heard Big Ed and The Dog begin to sing. Dimly, he could make out their outlines under the pearmain tree, and floating out over the spent cornfield came the dirge that rumbled from their throats, the lowest notes God made.

When Chris reached his bed, the whole thing, even life itself, seemed unutterably sad, and he wept long. The last good cry he ever had.

Twenty-three

LITTLE DOOTCHY was not seen in Schoodac District for going on a fortnight. When he did appear, it was at Clessie's store. The afternoon train had just gone through, and the mail had been sorted. The store was full of men and women doing the last errands of the day.

A dead silence fell when Little Dootchy entered. It wasn't his habit to patronize the local store, and folks wondered what he was up to now. Hostility fairly sizzled, but curiosity was hotter.

"Greetings, Mr. Peters," he called in his most unctuous voice. "See you got the whip back."

He laughed easily, as if the joke was on him and he didn't mind. His right hand was bandaged, but he appeared to use it naturally.

"What do you have in the way of cheese, Mr. Peters?"

"Hain't got nuthin' but rat cheese," Clessie said sullenly.

"Let me taste it. Ah, finest cheese in the world for cookery. Perhaps, shall we say, a little sharp to the tongue."

"Us folks like to taste our cheese."

"Excellent . . . excellent," said Little Dootchy, and laughed again as though some other joke, infinitely funnier, had been cracked. "And now I see you have a bolt of fine wool challis here," Little Dootchy resumed. "To my wife's taste, I'm sure."

Clessie got down the bolt of sprigged challis. "How much?" he asked.

"I might as well take the whole of it. Mrs. Duchesne's a big woman, you know." And again he laughed. He seemed pleased as Punch about everything.

"My wife was figgerin' to have herself a dress o' this," Clessie lied, hardly thinking what he said.

"Well, by all means... by all means. Half of it will do quite nicely, I suppose. Perhaps Mrs. Peters won't mind if my wife has a gown of the same stuff. Mrs. Duchesne goes out very little, you know."

"From what I hear, you be speakin' the plain truth fer oncet," somebody muttered aloud, but Little Dootchy found even this worthy of a complacent smile.

He wandered about the store, bowing to the ladies and greeting the men by their first names, while Clessie measured and cut the cloth, wondering the while how he could tell Prudence about the dress she was to have without bringing wrath about his ears.

Little Dootchy departed at last, his cheese and yard goods under his arm. Everyone in the store breathed deeply in relief. Clessie looked at the money the man had put down on the counter as if it would bite. "I'll be hornswoggled," he said to himself.

"Now what in merry hell do you suppose that was all about?" said Happy Tandy, who had left the post office unattended to see the show.

"Ast me, he ain't up to no good, he ain't."

" 'Judge not,' my friend," the minister spoke up.

Folks were not wont to answer back when their pastor spoke, but at the moment such distinctions didn't exist. "Judge, hell," the man responded. "I judge he's fixin' up some oncommon devilment. Me, I ain't trustin' him 's far's you could throw the bull that made that whip."

"Here, parson," Clessie said, raking the gold coins into his palm. "Take this fer... waal, to'ds that new organ you bin wantin'. Fer's I'm concerned, it's dirty earnt an' dirty spent. But I reckon a mite o' hymn music'll make it right."

"Up to no good" was everybody's conclusion, and Clessie, closing up the store a while later, felt he'd been having truck with the devil himself.

Twenty-four

FOR the better part of a month Little Dootchy kept the whole community on tenterhooks. His trips away from home were as frequent as before, but on the days when he was in Schoodac, he made a point of stopping off at the store, of giving his custom to local enterprises, such as they were. A new glove factory had been set up on the banks of the river, and it was known that he ordered a dozen pair of gauntlets, made to his own specifications. And from the sawmill over at Joppa he purchased white pine boards, about enough, Enoch Morrison, the sawyer said, to put up a privy.

"He be a-tryin' to soften us folks up fer somethin'," Happy Tandy concluded. "Reckon he don't rightly know the cussed grain o' the wood we're made on."

"Little pipsqueak!" Siah Peavy added. "Likes his beef rotten. Likes hisself a mite maggoty. Faugh!"

"A man ain't got no way to judge other folks, lessen by hisself," was David Mason's comment.

Now and then, in his journeys around the country, Little Dootchy took his wife with him. Clessie had taken a length of the challis home, and to his wife's amazement, he had suggested that she call in the village sempstress to help with the dress.

"Whatever's got into you, Clesson?" his wife wanted to know. She was obviously primed for a quarrel.

"Jest reckon I want him to see my wife can dress with the best."

"You men! I have a notion to make the stuff into a nightshirt. It don't seem right to embarrass her."

" 'Taint likely she'll be seein' it. But I want you should come over to the store someday when he's there. The way he spoke! 'S if no one on God's earth could come up to him and his'n! I got me a good-lookin' woman, too, Prudence, an' I aim to show him." Clessie felt rather proud of himself for this last, not having paid Prudence such a compliment since the days of their courtship. And it was true: Prudence was indeed a good-looker, and she was assuredly Clessie's wife. He thought himself a lucky man.

But Little Dootchy had taken his half of the bolt of goods down to Boston, and the dress he brought back to his wife might have come right out of a Paris salon. Its ruffles were piped with scarlet velvet to match the scarlet hearts of the rose sprigs, and at neck and wrist was exquisite handmade lace, as delicate as spider web. The hat that matched it was a confection of such simple elegance that Miss Nathan, who served the community's needs for a milliner, went straight home upon seeing it, in order to copy it, but she found she had no way of understanding that hat.

One midday Clessie heard the clippity-clop of the Duchesne bays going down the depot road, and sent a youngster over for his wife. Poor Prudence. When she came into the store, red of face from having put up peaches all the morning, rough of hand, and fearful of making a spectacle of herself, even Clessie could see he'd probably managed to make a fool of himself.

The bays clipped up to the hitching rail. Too late, Clessie saw that Little Dootchy had brought his wife along.

Judith sat her seat like a princess, her scarlet-gloved hands folded in her lap.

"Come on, git out," Little Dootchy commanded.

"I have no reason to," she replied.

"I said . . ."

If Prudence Peters's face was red, Judith Duchesne's was pale with her composed emotions. The two women met at the counter, their dresses as unlike as the common material allowed.

Prudence's face turned redder, and she tried to hide her hands. But Judith came up to her, holding out an ungloved palm. "I'm so glad to see you again, Mrs. Peters," she said, her graciousness like all sweet-melting things. "Ever since the day of the picnic, I've wanted to get your receipt for that piccalilli. I don't suppose you could give it to me this minute, but perhaps you'll write it down and send it to me."

"Why, Miz Duchesne, that old receipt has come down in my family for goodness knows how long. I could speak it in my sleep. You take a peck o' green tomatoes an' salt 'em down good overnight. Then, in the mornin', you wash the salty water off. Then you make a little bag o' spices . . . oh, a pinch o' this, a pinch o' that . . . you know."

Judith's laughter, light and lovely, rang all around the store. "Dear me, Mrs. Peters," she said. "I'm afraid I couldn't remember all that. I'm not as good a cook as you women here. I'd have to have it all put down on paper."

"Well, I tell you what, Miz Duchesne. You come right on over to my house. It's jest across the street. I got it writ down somewheres. Reckon I can put my hands right on it."

The two rose-sprigged challis dresses marched out of the store and across the street, chattering from flounce to flounce.

"An' what c'n I do for you?" Clessie asked, butter all over his tongue.

Little Dootchy must have heard the snickers at his back. Happy Tandy said later the man took one quick look at the whip, but that might have been Happy's imagination.

"I'll have a pound of sixpenny nails, and some hinges."

"Hear you're puttin' up a new backhouse, Mr. Duchesne," someone ventured. "Three-holer?"

"How 'bout a good stout lock?" Clessie suggested.

Little Dootchy rallied himself. A look of triumph came over his face. "No, my good neighbors," he said, altogether too pleasantly, "this outhouse will not require a lock. But, come to think of it, I'll need a chain. As you put it, sir, a good stout chain."

Clearly, the encounter was a draw. The two women could be seen coming back, and Little Dootchy hurried out to meet them.

"Jumpin' Jehoshaphat!" Happy Tandy exclaimed, as he watched Judith Duchesne handed up into the buggy, "Don't tell me he's agoin' to chain her to it!"

"Blessed if I know," Clessie said.

Two days later, as gaudy September threw her Joseph coat over the shoulders of the hills, Little Dootchy came down to meet the afternoon train from Boston. The usual village loafers were hanging around. Mike O'Shea, the town drunk, leaned, in a picturesque haze, against the depot wall. Happy Tandy was there with a mail sack. And Clessie, expecting a consignment of goods, having left the store in Prudence's care, sat on the baggage truck jawing with Willie Pike.

The train was late, as usual. Little Dootchy paced the platform, greeting all comers with a high unpleasant squall that seemed to be meant for laughter. In one hand he carried the ox chain.

"Looks as pleased with hisself as an old maid at a screwin'," Willie Pike said to Clessie.

A light dawned on Clessie. "I might o' knowed it . . . I might have knowed it," he said over and over.

"Knowed what, Clessie?"

"Never you mind. Jest you wait and see."

The engine came around the bend, blowing its whistle, and ground to a stop, a baggage car and one coach behind.

Eben Peaslee jumped for the baggage car to help unload. He had no more than got his footing than he turned, as though frightened of something, and fell sprawling on his hands and knees on the platform.

Little Dootchy roared, but over his laughter was heard a grimmer sound. The baggage man himself jumped down from the car. Sweat ran down his face.

"Who in hell belongs to that devil in there? By God, I've had him all the way up from Boston, an' this job ain't worth another minute o' the sight o' him."

Little Dootchy swaggered up, his flat backsides giggling. The baggage man boosted him into the car.

When he came out, minutes later, he led by the chain the ugliest bulldog a human being ever laid eyes on.

"Holy Mother o' God," Mike O'Shea yowled, flattening himself against the wall.

"That does her." Clessie muttered. "I thought as much."

The bulldog had not enjoyed his trip. He braced his legs, and Little

Dootchy was barely man enough to get the beast into his buggy. He got no offers of help. It was hard to tell, said Willie Pike, which was the meanest looking.

The rest of the baggage was unloaded in silence. The train pulled out for Joppa. A raw September wind came up and devil danced.

"Storm comin' up," someone opined.

"Yep. Some kind o' storm."

The day shuddered into her cloak of dusk.

Twenty-five

THE piazza of Clessie's store was crowded beyond capacity that night. Men filled the three steps that ran its length, and Clessie, waving his bamboo fan in time to his thoughts, now slow, now furious, held court.

On his way home, Little Dootchy had stopped off at Doc Gotchie's, ostensibly to have him take a look at one of his horses' hocks, but with the apparent purpose of regaling him with talk of the Bull, as he was afterward known to all.

"That bulldog," he had said, nodding with pride at the beast, "can lick anything in sight. I've spent a pretty penny having him trained. Want to make a bet on him?"

"Bet on what?"

"You know damned well there's only one dog in these parts worthy of his mettle."

"Fixin' to fight him, huh?"

"I don't aim to be murdered by any creature trespassing on what's mine. It'll be a fair scrap, right out in the open. I figure Peters can hold the betting money."

Doc told his friends if that all-fired great brute hadn't been right there, straining at his chain, he'd have beat Little Dootchy to a pulp without further ceremony. But Doc had a good idea of what the Bull was like. His chest muscles looked as hard as oak knots, and his eyes were killer eyes.

"I'll swear by The Dog," Doc nonetheless said.

"And bet on him, too?" Little Dootchy asked.

"I ain't a bettin' man. Reckon you won't find many as is."

"We'll see . . . we'll see. There's a mite of sporting blood in most of us. And if I figure you Yankees right, you don't aim to put money on a losing proposition."

Word got around quickly, as Little Dootchy knew it would. By supper time, it had reached as far as Burnhap District, and Clessie had seen fit to send word over to Schoodac for Big Ed to keep The Dog somewhere safe.

As evening came on, men came from every direction, and the hitching rail was full up with rigs. The full complement of sawmill men, most of them Canadian woodsmen, wandered in, as did the whole crew of men who had come with the glove factory.

"So that's why he's been goin' 'round, tryin' to butter us up," Clessie was thinking. "Fixin' to collect a piece o' cash. On Our Dog! Why, the consarned little whippersnapper!"

"It's a shittin' shame," Willie Pike said, as though he could read Clessie's mind.

"Watch your tongue, Willie," Clessie said, in deference to Clara Pickens, who walked by at that moment. "There's ladies present."

"Aw, it's only Clara. She's heard a sight wuss'n that from me."

Clessie didn't doubt that. Everyone knew that Clara Pickens survived—rather meagerly, to be sure—by harlotry. And no one was in the mood for joshing.

"Waal, be you goin' ter hold the money, Clessie?"

" 'Twarn't that I know that puny son of a sea dog were downright serious 'bout this, I'd stick his dirty money..." Clessie began, then changed his tack. "Waal, anyways, ef'n he aims to git The Dog, he's goin' ter keep tryin' till he does, an' it's best to have it happen where we can keep an eye out. Mebbe we c'n think up somethin'. You boys got any ideas?"

No one had any ideas.

"Can't tell Big Ed nothin'," Happy Tandy remarked. "He jest don't seem to savvy."

" 'Twon't do no good to keep The Dog tied up. This cuss can wait. An' wait. An' if we try anything on that bloody fool, he'll sic the Bull onto Ed. Reckon he's aimin' at Ed, anyways. Leastways, this way we can help Ed out."

There was a tremendous silence.

"Waal, be it so, Clessie. Here's my money," Willie Pike said, emptying his pockets. "On The Dog."

"I'll double that, on the bulldog," said one of the sawyers, waving several bills in front of Clessie's face. Another sawyer stood just behind with money at the ready.

"Hold on a mite," Clessie said. "This thing's goin' ter be done fair an' square, bein' it's got to be done at all. Anyone bettin' step into the store an' put your name down 'longside the amount he's paid in."

Little Dootchy was half right. There are a few gamblers, even a salting of semiprofessional ones, in any community. The pros put their bets on the Bull. But there were at least as many who bet on The Dog. And Clessie refused to accept a penny unless a man put his name down clear in pen and ink, for all to see.

The betting began slowly, a few coppers here, a crumpled two-dollar bill, one lone fiver. But on the third day, money began pouring in. Little Dootchy, leading the Bull by a short chain, swaggered into the store and placed a hundred dollars casually on the counter.

"Don't want to bet too high on a sure thing," he said. "Not sporting."

Siah Peavy, just come from dickering with a cattle buyer for his team of oxen, took one good look at the money he'd been paid for them, and put his hundred down beside Duchesne's.

"Triple that," Little Dootchy said, bringing out a sheaf of bills.

"Can't," said Siah Peavy, and walked out.

"God Almighty," said Clessie.

The town was split square in two. Good churchmen, who had never been known to take a chance on a quilt at the County Fair, laid bets on The Dog. Prudence Peters marched into the store one afternoon in high dudgeon, holding a cracker jar in one hand. She emptied it onto the counter, saying, "That's all my egg money. I don't rightly know why we're doing this. To my way o' thinkin', 'twould be a sight better not to let 'em have the satisfaction o' bettin' at all. But here it is. I guess we can't let Big Ed down, that's all."

The menfolks hadn't thought of this, and it was too late now to stop. Clessie put both his twenty-dollar gold pieces on The Dog. There were hot arguments in the night as to the relative merits of size and native strength against skill and young muscle, for it was reckoned the Bull was younger by years than The Dog. But what it added up to was loyalty, pure and simple.

Little Dootchy went around bragging, his little moustache primped to two sabre points. He swore he'd get that big black son of a bitch if it was the last act of his life, and he more than hinted that it would be no concern of his if The Dog's master got hurt in the fray. No skulking lout of a country numbskull was going to hang around his wife. Not and get away with it.

Two weeks passed. In Schoodac, the menfolks went about their work with set jaws. Bart Jewell sat by the hour oiling up his six-shooters and throwing his lass rope over the heads of anything that came in sight with a head.

"Jest practicin'," he said, catching his nephew by one foot, sprawling him flat on the ground.

As for Chris, he scarcely slept at all, for trying to figure out some way to help his friend. His mother suggested a camping trip, up to the

top of Kearsarge, to get Big Ed out of the way. But Ed's father, trying to
pick his own apples to save his neighbors the trouble, twisted his bad
leg, and infection set in, keeping him down in bed again. No one could
have made Ed leave his father anyway.

Mary Jewell had decided not to trouble Judith with the affair, but
Judith brought the subject up herself. "I'm sorrier than I can say," she
sighed. "I have tried everything I know, but nothing will stop him. He
only . . ."

"Yes, I know. He takes it out on you," Mary said. "Never you
mind. Leave it alone. Somehow I can't believe but what The Dog can
take care of himself. I . . . I even pray about it, Judith, though goodness
knows what the good Lord thinks of praying for a dog."

"Remember the sparrow, Mary."

"It would half kill Ed, if anything should happen to The Dog."

"Yes, he knows that, too. That's the sad part. He's just obsessed
about Ed. I don't know what he'll stop at."

Little Dootchy marched into the store on a Tuesday morning,
rubbing his palms together in satisfaction. "Well, boys, guess I've got
my animal in condition. Had to get him used to me, you know. How
about this coming Saturday? They'll be down to the store that
afternoon."

By noon of Saturday, there was no room left on the hitching rail for
another halter rope, and some of the rigs had to be put into the church
sheds. Factory and sawmill were closed down for the afternoon. Over
the century that the little village had lain peacefully under its elms and
maples, it had been witness to no such gathering. Clara Pickens, who
kept herself pretty well out of sight in her little house down by the
river, came right out and took a place on the post office steps. The rest of
the womenfolks stayed at home, but the lace curtains in all the houses
along the street could be seen moving apart, slyly.

Chris had told Mr. Cheney about the affair, hoping he would try to
keep Big Ed at home.

"There ain't no use, boy," Ed's father told him. "If it don't happen
this week, it'll happen next. I plumb can't do a thing about it. Anyways,

I reckon he'll come out all right, some way."

Bart Jewell put on his cowboy hat and strapped his six-shooters around his waist, and even William didn't say much in reproof.

"Don't get yerself into trouble, Bart. Killin's a state prison offense here in the east, yer know," was all he said.

Little Dootchy had the sense of timing of a showman. He drove up one end of Maple Street just as the wheaten thatch of Ed's head showed at the other end. Folks barely had time to notice, with amazement, that he had brought his wife with him, too.

Ed had just reached the bottom of the steps to the store when Little Dootchy, saying nothing, unleashed the Bull. The Dog wasn't looking.

"Hey, by God, that ain't fair," someone shouted.

But the Bull had The Dog by the throat. The Dog braced his great legs and made a terrible shaking, but the Bull held on.

"Dod!" Ed yelled, a vast puzzlement reddening his face.

But The Dog only bared his teeth. His eyes were as red as the wrath of God.

"By God, he ain't goin' to fight!"

"Sic 'im, Dog! Sic 'im!"

"Dod!" Ed cried piteously, the tears streaming down his face "DOD!"

But The Dog only braced and waited. Suddenly it seemed as if everyone was on The Dog's side. They all shouted at once.

Willie Pike let out a string of oaths and started for Little Dootchy, who stood on the steps, his legs spread wide, a smile on his face. But someone held Willie back. Bart Jewell slipped one of his guns from its holster.

"Holy God, somebody do something!"

"Clessie, go git some cayenne pepper!"

Then it all happened in one burst of crazed ferocity. With a roar like the bull of Bashan, Big Ed hurled himself into the fray. There was no telling dogs from man. Blood and hair and frenzy cluttered the ground. Clara Pickens screamed like a banshee. Horses reared and thrashed. Only Little Dootchy stood quite still, a runnel of spit drooling down his chin.

No longer would any man say Big Ed was simple. He got the Bull by the testicles and sank his teeth in as far as they would go. In the split of a hair, the Bull let go The Dog, and turned on Ed. But before anyone could see what had happened, The Dog got the Bull by the neck and hurled him clean into the middle of the street, dead.

The village square fell silent as the grave. White and bitter, Little Dootchy stood over the carcass of his dog. Happy Tandy wept big silent tears into his beard. Clessie Peters unashamedly wiped his eyes.

Judith Duchesne sat, as she had sat throughout the proceedings, upright and remote on the seat of the buggy. She was garmented in gray, belly high with child, and the folds of her skirt were carved granite over her knees. One crimson plume of her picture hat cupped lovingly under an ear, picking up the first scarlet maple leaves drifting, unheeding, onto the street. Her eyes appeared to dwell on the hills yonder, and her hands were folded one over the other in her lap. It was as if a statue of serenity had been carved out of the exquisite texture of all her being. Chris Jewell, who watched her almost as attentively as he had the fight, said later that only once did a muscle of her move. At the moment the bulldog fell, she relaxed for the space of a breath, and became human again.

Big Ed picked himself up and spat. He put out one hand and quieted The Dog. Then, looking neither right nor left, he retrieved his jug and went into the store, Clessie following.

"My paw, he wants a mite o' salt pork an' some 'lasses."

Little Dootchy had driven off, leaving his dog in the middle of the street. The store was quickly mobbed with chattering men.

"Yore paw, Ed," Clessie said loudly, to make himself heard, "can have the whole damned store, if that be what he wants."

Ed only grinned. He really hadn't taken it all in.

"Tlessie," he said, "mebbe you dot a bone . . . fer my dod."

Clessie brought out a quarter of beef. "Ladies an' gentlemen," he said. "A standin' roast of beef, prime."

He cut a hunk of meat as big as a peck measure, amidst the guffaws of his audience.

Willie Pike spoke up. "Christ," he said, "I'm fair happy I ain't got ter crawl inter bed with him tonight."

Clessie fetched a bottle out from under the counter. The village began to celebrate.

Twenty-six

THE clocks along the Brook struck two.

Two o'clock, the hour when demons walked. The eagle on his bough atop Kearsarge rolled the loaded dice of his dream in his throat, and started up a frightened chorus of undercreatures. The Brook, beneath its overhang of trees, had darkened since the set of the old moon, becoming a running shroud adown the mountainside. Black, black, the hands that beat the drum of the earth, and Fear walked unlet.

Willie Pike's words had been repeated. They lay like stones within the belly, pressing against breast and loin.

Old Iddo Myrick awoke. His fingers searched the long unheeded private place, and one sweet sigh of old forgotten desire leaped weakly before he fell back into sleep.

"There was a time," little Sarah Peavy thought, stirring to half consciousness, "when Siah an' me . . . we did the thing night after night. A time when he'd come in to dinner an' we'd lock the chamber door, to keep the younguns out . . . an' the dinner gittin' cold on the stove. It were before . . ." But, there, she had just clean forgotten how or why it had ended. Slowly, slowly, had come the lonesomeness, the drag. She put her peaked face up to the night air, making weather with her lean nose, and dreamed of a tall dark man, with waxed moustache, who stood before her, both hands fumbling in his pockets, his legs spread wide . . .

Siah waked full up. The first time, almost, in memory, that he had come awake erect. He made no move, but let the vision bloom, full flower. Under his palm, uprisen nipples blew, all rose, and he felt the flesh again, the miracle of ample flank, and the beauty, incredible, of hair. A thrush upon her branch outside drew her head from underneath a wing and let flow the poem Siah might have tried to make had he not been Siah. The petals of his flower wilted, fell limp. Anger came.

Saphronia Goss was talking in her sleep when she awoke. She often did, at two in the morning. Now she was wide awake. She could hear the hens, restive on their roost, and the old collie biting endlessly at his mange, now and then growling at something passing in the night. Saphronia remembers Willie's words, and rising on one elbow, looks long at the humped-up figure of her husband. Nothing could wake Bertie Goss. Thunder and fire he had been known to sleep through, and cries of visiting colic babes, and the voice of a cow lamenting the loss of her calf. Saphronia remembered Bertie now. So many years, she hasn't remembered him, except to din words into his ears. Bless me, she thought, he wasn't what I wanted for a man. Honest, I don't know what he sees in me, either, to tell the truth. I'd ruther, sometimes, that I had a man would slap me down. I could o' stood a licking now an' then. Better by far then his pat, pat on my butt. Bertie's a good man, now I come to think on it, and I ain't done him right, noways. He's safe, if that be anything to crow on, an' I guess it be, come time one's old. I could of gone out west with him that time, hadn't I been too ornery to stir. I guess I really wanted him to go, an' leave me here to have my whole way of things. It's downright strange, it be, the wickedness is in us wimmen, times. Look at him now. Saphronia looked at him, and something nearer warmth for Bertie came into her than had come since many, many years, but a different warmth. Older and better, as if it had been put by to ripen in the wood. "Dear Heavenly Father," Phronie prayed, touching the wisps of hair around Bertie's bald spot, "make me a better wife to him while there's still time. He's got that pain he don't much talk about, an' it may not be too long away now. I don't like hasty puddin', never did. But that don't mean I can't beat up a batch for him.'' And, thinking of all the days upon days upon days when she had racked her brain to think up anything to cook but hasty pudding, Phronie wept. Bertie, responding to something deeply unconscious, reached out his hand and patted her ass. She had to clench her hands to keep from smacking him.

Bart Jewell came off his horse, head first, landing, to his dismay, in his bed in Schoodac. He'd been performing on that pinto stud again. Under the eucalyptus by the shack in the arroyo, the black-haired Mexican girl was nursing her sickly child and watching him. Only a couple of nights before, he'd caught her going out to meet the slender Indian boy under the willows. She had stood stolid, with her ebony eyes a challenge to his manhood. But he was a New Hampshireman and couldn't beat her for her offense. Oh, he'd called her names, all right. Yes, plenty of names. He thought if he could ride the young stallion right, she'd have to give him her admiration, at least. But just then the Indian boy had come along, riding the range, and he was part horse and part man, going by at one of those easy-looking lopes. Dolores took her eyes off Bartholomew Jewell and never put them back again. It wasn't in the cards, that's all. But he had never again looked on white flesh. He guessed it looked . . . well, in some way, not quite well done. As if the flesh itself had never learned anything. Bart drew down the end of the bolster and threw one leg over it. Presently he heard a coyote yowl, and he smiled. In his dream was long black hair, and two women, one of them paleface.

Mary Jewell heard the grandfather clock by the stairway in the front hall strike the hour. The huge log that was her husband stretched crosswise of the bed, leaving her only a corner. She knew just what would happen if she tossed and wakened him. She couldn't bear that burden this night. God knew, she'd borne it long and patiently enough, ever since she was seventeen and the first shock of it had killed something in her. By now she was well practiced in forbearance of her wifely duty. Sometimes she'd put her mind on one thing, sometimes another, keeping her wide eyes on a crooked streak on the ceiling, where rain had leaked in. Oftenest she thought of little Myrtle, the elder of her two daughters, both now dead. How she had laughed, or put her palms against her mother's cheeks, or of the night she died. Of what it would be like to have her now, a girl, a womankind. Even that was better than the other thing. Well, tonight, she'd just slip out and boil up some sassafras tea, and stay up. But the moment she moved, an arm was thrown across her, and it was too late. She sighed. She thought of Judith Duchesne, and what happened to herself ceased to matter as much. It would soon be over, anyhow, and then she would have her tea. She fixed her eyes on the streaked ceiling, and suddenly thought of John. Thinking of him and Judith, she scarcely felt the thrust of her husband, feeling rather the vast sorrows of a world in which Christian love, under the clear mandate of God, could have been brought to blindness and defeat.

In the great canopied spool bed downstairs in the front chamber, Judith Duchesne awoke. Peace drew the feather of its wing across the dark, as a dove rising in the fog. Something not seen. Smitten and spent, a nothingness of unbeleaguered rest had come. The events of the day and evening past had left no trace on her memory. She only knew that here, in sanctuary, she had remitted evil. Between the hot hill that had been yesterday, and tomorrow's unsigned signature, she floated on the sweet glad of now. There was something she had left far, far behind, and something else far, far ahead. But now she walked beside the Brook, and another walked beside. She could not see a face, only the light that shone from it and rocked her spirit with a fartherness and otherness. She had no body, but somewhere long, long ago. She was not a woman anymore, and he not man. She did not need the touch, the word, for everywhere was song and fingering. 'This must be God,' she thought. 'I have come through.'

And even when, awake again, she did remember the events that led up to leaving her husband's bed, the sordidness was gone, and she felt whole as she had never felt wholeness before. Nothing, indeed, had touched her. She had drunk the wine he poured for her, in sacrament, body and blood. Faintly she saw, as in a drawing on the palimpsest of her time, herself, standing all in white as he commanded, her hair soughing the shoulders of the night, while he reviled and persecuted. Passive under the onslaught of his words, his hands, his lash, she bided. Behind the silver birch outside, the sickle moon lay waiting for Venus to come to him, and one tiny star laughed a knowing laugh. The cross on which she hung had loving arms, and in the white white agony, she died, and rose again in farthest deluges of joy that nothing ever in the world again could harm.

Now she stood upon the hill where stars are born, and cast one glance back into the abyss, seeing the shell of Woman there, white clad and cold, emptied of everything. It went from her, the dread chasm of her yesterdays, passing dream without memory, remote, remoter, lost, until the very crevasse itself turned rainbow shine, and all the panoply of virgin hues, newly brushed from His own hand upon her soul, flooded the earth.

To Judith came faintly the memory of her husband, drunk, standing before her, helplessness in his eyes, a whip at his feet. With shining, ineradicable power, she gazed at him, and he, stumbling, went up the stairs to his chamber, alone.

The memory spent itself even as it burgeoned. Judith smiled. She had come through upon some other side, guerdoned, untouchable, renewed. She would sleep well now. But, turning a little where she lay, she felt a sharp needle of pain at the base of her spine.

Old Sabina had just come in from wandering. She had slept a little earlier in the night, on the verge of the marsh, where she had gone to gather the tall thoroughwort. Her pinched and ancient buttocks were still wet. Then, remembering a stand of sassafras up Salisbury way, she'd taken up her basket and gone to fetch some bark. Somewhere along the way, she'd taken a lithe, protesting froglet in her palm, more for coolness of it than that she believed any virtue in the spew of frogs. Now, she put it in the sink, and pumped up water for it, before sitting wearily in her rocking chair, rocking to the rhythm of the wind outside, and mouthing at a mildewed slab of bread from the bare cupboard. She was all wakefulness tonight, and had both ears cocked for the telling she was sure was in the wind. Of late, her listening had dulled a good deal, and in her heart, she yearned for the voices which had been dear to her. All too frequently, now, she was a girl again, and when she reached for root and simple, a huge black hand would pluck it for her and put it in her basket, whereupon she would kiss the hand and dance as with young feet around its vanishing. Or when the wind came up, and in it the first syllables of divine speech, strong gleaming arms would take her, enfold her, smothering sound and sight of earth, leaving her vision but one blazoned horizon, just a step away, where all horizons meet.

She poked up a meager fire, placing faggots crosswise according to her plan, and put her kettle on, dropping a pinch of one thing and another into the boil and brew. With the first sip, a smoke flew back into her eyes, and somewhere in her loins she felt a thrust of pain, not hers. In it was a foretelling. She snatched up her shawl and ran outdoors.

The clocks along the Brook struck three.

Mary Jewell, resolved against further sleep that night, dressed and went downstairs. She couldn't keep her mind off Judith, noways. After she had downed three cups of good strong tea, she cast about in her mind for something to do that would please William. It was her way to make some gesture of immolation for her lack of wifeliness. She glanced at the clock and calculated that if she hurried about it, there would be just time to whip up a steamed brown bread for breakfast, his favorite morning food. She built up the dying fire and set out her makings on the kitchen table. Then she lit a lantern, took up a pan and a flour sieve, and started for the barn for two cups of corn meal from the bin.

At first the shadow flitting on the road looked like an enormous cat riding the broomstick of the wind, but Mary quickly knew it for what it was. "Sabina," she called. "Sabina Dow, what are you up to at this time of night?"

Sabina came within the circle of lantern light. She held up to Mary's view a tiny sack, fashioned of some soft skin and tied with something that looked like old dried gut.

Her voice was dire and drone: "Ar spae un thole, waes me, waes me, awauken i' thar wind. Walie, walie." She rubbed one hand around her belly, wailing softly.

"Where are you bound for?" Mary asked, her voice sharp with trouble and vexation.

Sabina pointed in the direction of the Duchesne house. "Ar unco sune, thair bairntime, coom." She passed her hand across her face, as though she tried to remember some half-forgotten thing. "Swith water flow, wanrestfu' by Awee, awee, ar be, un bairn. Awee. Ar hear un blether bizzard blawn about. Aback, aback, for's glaum un bairn, ye hatefu' bird fro' yon Auld Hornie's nest. Aback...aback!"

Her lamentation fell into the night breeze like the utterance of all winds at once, a sudden flaw that sent the dust flying and wimpled all the trees. Then, sudden, stilled.

"Nae mair . . . nae mair," Sabina breathed. "Nae mair I ken . . . nae mair. Un teat o' auld foretellin', an' a', a' agone."

It was the saddest sound, Mary thought, she had ever in her life heard. Sabina folded down like a tired child, holding her bag of medicine against her heart as a child holds a rag doll with all the sawdust gone.

"Go home to bed, Sabina," Mary said softly. And even as she spoke, Sabina turned homeward.

It was too late now for the brown bread, Mary thought, even if she hurried; hot saleratus biscuits would do almost as well. Besides, her heart was very troubled now. That man could have killed Judith by this time, and no one would know. She drew a shawl around her shoulders and passed quietly along the Brook. When she came to the willow tree, she heard Little Dootchy snoring. She circled the house, but no light shone, and she heard no sound but the regular rasp and scrunch from upstairs.

"I don't care," she said aloud as she regained her own grounds, "I'm going there, come day. It can't be right, to leave her there like this. It can't be *right*."

T wenty-seven

T HE day, full blossom, came at last. Nothing along the Brook was the same as yesterday. All felt the difference. The fitful blasts of wind, toward dawn, had covered the ground with a fresh layer of leaf. A counterfeit of spring was in the air, in color and in sound. The white birches, softly yellowing, wore leaflet hue, and something in the light, some mellow tone, had put upon the cornstalks on the uplands the brightest green of the year, as if they had but sprouted from their spears. Birdsong was muted to the lilt of lullaby, and only the abundance of goldenrod and asters gave evidence of the failing year.

Phronie Goss waited for Bertie to come in from the barn. Sugared doughnuts waited under a cloth in the warming oven, and when she saw the long rent he'd made in his shirt while struggling to get the old rooster back in his pen, she bit her tongue and fetched him another shirt. Siah Peavy, going out across the marsh to bring in a stray calf, had gathered a bunch of closed gentians for his wife. Even Bart Jewell, gloating over the triumph of The Dog, swallowed a whole cud of tobacco, trying to keep his Christ Almighties down.

William washed down his seventh biscuit with his fourth cup of coffee. "Mighty fine biscuits, Mrs. Jewell," he said. "See our neighbor took off right early this mornin'. Should think he'd never want to show his face in these parts again.''

"Let us pray,'' said his brother, piously. "By God—excuse me, Mary—by God, I wisht I had a rope as long as Schoodac Brook, with prickles onto it like thistle stalks, and pison into every pricker on't, an' I'd throw that ol' lass rope so tight around his neck, 'twould stink o' the carrion o' him s' far, the Devil himself would haf ter hold his nose.''

Mary stacked the unwashed breakfast dishes in the sink, and left them, an unheard-of act. She found Judith sitting by her kitchen table, drinking hot coffee. Mary scrambled in through a window.

"Are you all right this morning, Judith?''

"Oh, yes. I think I never felt so well.''

Indeed, Mary thought she had never seen her friend looking so well, though it was hard to say in just what way. She had a welt across her brow, but her eyes had changed. She seemed almost too lovely to set eyes upon, but Mary could see that she was tired. The light that came from her eyes dominated her. It came from far far back within, and it was as if they were no longer young eyes, certainly not the eyes of a girl in her twenties.

"I was a . . . a little afraid,'' Mary said, lamely. "I guess I didn't sleep any too well. I woke up sharp at two o'clock, thinking about you. I wasn't sleepy anymore, so I stayed up.''

Judith smiled. "I woke up at just that time, too,'' she said. "They say it's the hour of ghosts. But . . . I can tell you, Mary, there are no more ghosts. Sometime I'll tell you . . . if I may . . . what happened to me. No, I'm fine. I've been up since a little after three myself. I . . . I seem to have a little pain. Oh, it isn't much. It just keeps coming back.''

Mary's wits all gathered in a familiar focus. "Where is the pain?'' was her first question.

"Well, the first few times it came, it was way down in my lower spine. I guess I must have got . . . got a bit upset.''

"You have been having it since three o'clock?''

"Why, yes. Off and on.''

"Exactly what do you mean by 'off and on'?''

"Well, it comes on, quite sharp, and goes suddenly away, and it doesn't come again for quite a while."

"How often?"

"Why, I haven't noticed it that particularly. It will go away as the day wears on."

"Every half hour?"

"I guess so. About that, yes."

"Is it still in the lower part of your back?"

"Y . . . yes. It kind of goes through, towards the front. It's hard to tell, exactly. The baby's kicking so."

"Mmmmm . . . Judith, will you do something for me? Will you go back to bed this minute, and lie flat? I'm going to stand right here until you do. You don't need to tell me what happened to you last night. It isn't any of my business. But it is my business to see you don't get sick. I'm *making* it my business."

"But I haven't done any of my work . . . not last night's dishes, even."

"Last night's dishes will be right where you left them when you get feeling well enough," Mary assured her. "There probably isn't a thing wrong with you that lying still for a few hours won't cure. But I can tell you this, Judith Duchesne. I've put up with him long enough, and the way he treats you. And when I get my dander up, something is very likely to bust wide open. No. I'm not going to interfere with your business. But I'm not going to let you get sick in this house, either, and no one to know."

"All right," said Judith. "I guess I'll be glad to lie down. I'll get into the bed in the downstairs chamber, and you can see me through the front windows, if you're bound to."

"Don't drink any more hot things," Mary said, one leg over the window sill. "And try to sleep."

At eleven o'clock, with dinner simmering on the stove, Mary hurried over and tiptoed up onto the porch of the Duchesne house. Judith was sleeping. Her face, relaxed, was pale and youthful, incredibly lovely.

She isn't pretty at all, Mary thought. But she could see...well, she could understand how a man would...

At two in the afternoon she went over again, but came back instantly, running. She called Chris, and sent him to The Corners for Doc Sanborn. "I guess you'll have to go shanks' mare, son," she said. "Your father is clean off over Salisbury way with the team. Did your Uncle Bart go with him?"

"I don't think so," said Chris. "I think he's mowing the second crop in the south field."

"Well, stop by and tell him to come over to Mrs. Duchesne's. Tell him to bring a hatchet with him. I can get in through a window, but I'm not going to ask Doc Sanborn to. Tell Bart for me, he can hack down every door in that house if he's a mind to."

Before returning to Judith, Mary went for the satchel she kept against such times. She checked its contents: the rolls of soft old flannel; the bottle of spirits of niter; the pint of rum. Her face had come together in one node of purpose. It was clear to see that no one had better cross her path.

"Don't try to hold it in, child," Mary said, pushing back the dark hair where it sweated on the brow. " Scream, if you feel like screaming. It'll do the muscles good. It's relaxing. This isn't any time to be a lady."

The paroxysm passed, and both women laughed.

"That's right. Laugh and cry. That's the way of things. I'll fetch you another cup of nit'y tea."

Now was the first chance she'd had for a word in private with Doc Sanborn. She found him drinking from his bottle in the kitchen, This was a bad sign. It was said of Doc Sanborn that when he had the almost impossible to do, he did it sober, but when he tackled the impossible, he had to be roaring drunk.

"Mary Jewell," he said, "there jest ain't any reason on God's earth for her losin' that child, as I can see. But she's goin' to...an' by God she's goin' to do it the hard way. Christ, the child don't want to be born, but it's clean outer the womb. You ought to take a drop o' this yourself, Mary. It's going to be a long pull. Send the boy down to the village an' leave word with Cless I'll be up here. An' if some goddamn fool sees fit to get the pip, tell him to take a dose of castor oil.''

"How about *her?*" Mary asked.

"There's times when all a body can do, Mary, is the next thing to do. An' there's times like this when even an old codger like me, who's seen 'em come an' go nigh onto fifty years, an' had a fair amount o' luck, if I do say so myself, don't know from minute to minute what the next thing's goin' to be.''

"You can't fool me, Ellery Sanborn. I've seen you at your work too many times.''

"Yes, Mary. I'm an ornery old cuss, and that's for sure. An' you knew her, my wife, an' how she was a pulin' invalid all her life, for want o' the right care birthin' time. An' when I see a woman lyin' there in pain, it all comes back to me, an' there ain't much, I reckon, in those times, twixt me an' what Almighty God tells me to do next.''

He drew a long swig from his bottle. "Mary, you got any idea what's makin' this come on?''

"Yes, Ellery, I have. That's what I came out here to tell,'' Mary said firmly. "You've heard enough to know something about that . . . that husband of hers. He didn't want a child. He couldn't bear for her to have anything that would take her mind off him. Well, a few weeks ago, he tried to get her to take something to . . . to get rid of it, but she refused. I hate to think of what went on in this house last night, after that dog affair. But I found this when I came in this afternoon. She'd been too sick to wash up her dishes. Smell of it.''

She took a wineglass from the cupboard where she'd hidden it, a thimbleful of dregs in it.

The doctor took one sniff and hurled the glass across the room, where it splintered against the baseboard. "Jesus Christ,'' he said.

"She'd never have taken it, willingly. The good Lord knows, he's done enough wickedness to break any woman's spirit, but hers. When I first saw her this morning, she looked better than I've seen her, ever.''

"Often happens that way,'' muttered Doc Sanborn. He stood looking at the shattered glass. "Damn me for an old fool,'' he said.

"With that, we could have put him where he belongs, behind bars. An' now I've gone an' spilled the evidence. Well, Mary, I can depend on you. We'll do what we can."

The tallow candles spluttered in the bedroom, and the great eyes in the white face on the pillow flew like wild sea birds, scudding on an unknown shore. The Jewell brothers, Bart and William, had put together a rack, and Judith Duchesne lay on it, her feet resting on the footboard. The baby, pushing against unbroken membranes, thrashed continuously. A kind delirium closed down the shutters of reality, bringing instead a train of fancies, playthings to divert the sick mind and tortured body.

Phronie had brought over a chicken fricassee with dumplings for Mary and Doc Sanborn, and Sarah Peavy had come fetching a green-apple pie. After supper, Clessie had driven up with Prudence, bearing a crock of piccalilli and a spice cake. Bart helped himself generously to the pie and the cake, though he had been fed with usual abundance at home. He felt he deserved some small reward for having resisted the strong temptation to take Mary at her word, contenting himself with the removal of the hinges from the kitchen door.

Toward midnight, when no change in Judith's condition seemed likely for a time, the women sent their menfolks home. Phronie, restless, tried to find something she could do, but when the dishes had been washed and put away there seemed to be nothing else to do. The house was spotless. "Reckon I might as well make up a batch of bread," she said.

"Goodness, I don't think I could bring myself to cook anything," said little Sarah Peavy. " 'Twould seem too much like makin' fun'ral meats. You seen her mendin' basket 'round?"

"She keeps her mendin' in the bottom drawer o' the highboy, in the settin' room," Phronie informed her. "What you thinkin' about, Pru, so quiet like?"

"I'm prayin'," Prudence answered. "Don't fret me. I'm jest atalkin' with God. I . . . well, I'm askin' a special favor, bein' I think it's comin' to her."

"Waal, times, He seems downright onreasonable, ef'n ye ast me,"

Phronie said. "But don't, fer goodness sake, *ast* me. Ye can add my prayer to yer own. I reckon the Heavenly Father Hisself is sick o' my kecklin' by now."

Prudence looked up. She had been mentally saying her beads. She had been a Catholic before she married Clesson. "Times like this is queer, for sure," she said. "Here you be, Phronie, arter all these years, realizin' how yore tongue has ran on. An' only last night, suthin' woke me up tow'ds two in the mornin', and I got to goin' over my sins, I did. Kinder like a drowndin' man, as they say. I don't guess I ever 'preciated my Clesson, not rightly, all these thirty years. An' you know what, he woke right up, too. 'You 'wake, Pru?' he says. 'Ayah, I'm wide awake.' 'Well,' he says, 'I bin athinkin', Pru. That warn't a fair fight from the beginnin', the way he let that crittur o' his at The Dog withouten warnin' him fair. I'll git the boys together, an' let's we give all that money to the parson, fer that organ.' Ayah, things be muckle quair, as ol' Sabina would o' said."

"Funny, Sabina hain't showed up," Sarah said. "Mebbe a good sign."

"She did, though," Phronie corrected, dipping a wooden spoon into the lard pail. "Mary tol' me. I guess I got to hand it to Sabina, after all. She wuz aspiritin' about this mornin', talkin' somethin' o' bairn bein' born too soon."

"Holy Mary, Mother o' God," Prudence said under her breath. Aloud, she said, "Come to think on it, it's all fer her. Why, before she come here, with her fair pretty ways, there hadn't o' been more'n th'ordinary birthin' an' buryin' an' pickle makin' in this here town, sence I c'n remember. O' course, folks hanged theirselves or others, now an' then, an' there wuz little Bessie Fowler as wuz caught buryin' her baby in the barn cellar. But nothin' like Miz Duchesne. Us wimmen folks, we ain't too awful charitable to'ds one another, ef the truth be said. Allus agabbin' 'bout our neighbor's business. But here we are this minute, all bound together like them Siamese twins, an' every one of us aprayin' fer her good. That batch o' bread you're makin', Phronie, be some sort o' prayer. An' look at you, Sarah Peavy, mendin' *his* socks."

"Amen," Phronie murmured.

"Amen," the others responded.

Judith Duchesne put out one hand, icy with sweat, and tightened it on Mary's, hot with sweat. A long moan issued from her lips.

Doc Sanborn, standing at the foot of the bed, swaying a little on his feet, looked tired far beyond fatigue. His lips moved. "What next?" he asked within his humble soul. "Oh, Lord, what next?"

Chris had gone over to be with Big Ed. But he found that his friend wasn't with anyone that night. The two boys sat under the apple tree beside the grave of the fawn, and clearly, Ed's mind was far away somewhere, beyond the boundaries of any earth Chris Jewell was acquainted with. Over and over he kept saying words, whole phrases, sentences. They would have been familiar enough from any other man, being about the things that had happened to him during the turns of the seasons they had been together. But coming from Ed, they had a pure unearthliness, as if the ox, the felling of the trees, the fish in the Brook, were somehow translated, and had the strangeness of all foreign things.

They could see the Duchesne kitchen, and the women moving about. They saw Doc Sanborn and Chris's mother coming and going. They could hear, faintly, the keening of Judith's travail.

Suddenly, Big Ed got to his feet and strode rapidly toward the Duchesne house, not so much as pausing at the Brook. The Dog was at his heel, and Chris ran along behind. When Ed reached the house, he went right through the kitchen door, across the kitchen, and into the front bedroom.

Doc Sanborn opened his mouth to object, but Mary Jewell made a sign, and he desisted. "This next," he thought. "Whatever you say, merciful One."

Ed looked down at the closed face of the woman on the bed. "Tome, Dod," he whispered, "Let's us sing. Soft now."

And they sang:

I brought a little deer fer you.
Breathe easy now.
Now little deer, don't fret yerself.
Yer only hearin' footsteps in the dark.
Yer mother, she ain't very far.
They be her footsteps comin' back fer you.
Thar be a great hand guidin' her to you.
Her little titties are all full o' milk.
Jest hold on a second, little deer.
She's got an ol' rough tongue.
'Twill lap the blood away.
Breathe easy, now . . . jest easy, easy, easy.
Thar God up in the sky, He's got His eye sharp out fer you.
Breathe easy, now.
Thar God, He make the speckles on yer hair.
He make yer pretty ears, all soft an' tall.
He put the light o' lovin' in yer big brown eyes.
He put the lovin' heart in the ol' ox.
He put a flake o' snow soft over yer.
He fill yer mother's titties up with milk.
He fix the moon up in His sky to shine down here.
He put the beatin' heart inside o' you.
Breathe easy now.
Breathe easy now.

Judith opened her troubled eyes, and saw Ed kneeling by her. The Dog had put his paws on the white counterpane, and his head rested between them. Of eiderdown and milkweed baby angels' tongues, their song was made. Of little titties full of milk, and tiny beating hearts. Of starry flakes of snow upon the face, and the rough tongue of love.

Judith put out her hand. It rested lily white on the shaggy head of The Dog, and Big Ed looked at it. His tears fell on it.

Tears started up in Judith's eyes. Slowly, she began to cry. A light of faint hope came into Doc Sanborn's eyes. Her body now shook with sobbing. When the next spasm came, she screamed as she had not before.

Doc Sanborn pushed Big Ed aside, while Mary Jewell took both of Judith's hands within her own, and pressed her face down on the agony.

The dawn comes slowly over the autumn fields of New Hampshire. The hoarfrost plays upon every blade of grass, making separate spears to pierce the coming sun. The windfalls on the ground are rimmed with white, and the cattle in the high pastures huddle together in the harrying wind. The joe-pye weed trembles its dry stalks.

Mary placed the small dead child in Phronie's arms, and hurried back to do for her who still lived, though faintly, precariously. She and Doc worked in silent urgency to bring the afterbirth. Doc was just drunk enough. His old pinched hands, holding the buttocks with one, and massaging the belly with the other, worked in a rhythm that was like a dance, over and back, over and back, and his whole body swayed in time. Mary, feeling the all-too-weak pulse, called out for hot wet cloths, and the three women in the kitchen produced them in a matter of minutes.

Sarah Peavy kept the kettle boiling, handing the empty water buckets to Big Ed, who kept silent vigil on the door rock. Prudence Peters had fumbled about in the highboy drawers and found a length of outing flannel among the baby things. She sat in her corner, audibly telling her beads, as she sewed a tiny shroud. Phronie, her wisps afly, had put on a dust cap, and was kneading bread. It was like the rhythm of the doctor's kneading, over and back, over and back, the wrists turning.

With the placenta came the blood.

"Jesus, she can't afford to lose all this blood," Doc exclaimed. "Hand me that roll of cotton, Mary, quick ... quick."

Mary, anxiously watching the dead-white face on the pillow, handed over the roll of cotton. As she did so, she heard the rattle of wheels on the loose planks of the bridge.

"Oh, Lord in heaven," she said. "It's him. He's coming home ... her husband."

Sweat fell from the doctor's face as he stuffed the cotton in. "Go tell them women out there, if he so much as shows his face at this door, I'll kill him dead, by God I will."

Little Dootchy must have seen the lights burning in the kitchen, and Big Ed coming back from the well house with the buckets. Whatever he saw, he chose to come to the house by the back way, so that he would not be seen until he was practically at the door.

Ed had dumped the buckets and was standing on the door rock in the glooming of the day. The moon, tipping down over the headpiece of Kearsarge, vied with the crafty lift of earliest day. Chris, coming up from the Brook, where he had taken a plunge, saw Little Dootchy and Big Ed meet. He saw a metallic glint, and knew at once it came from a pistol. A shot rang out. Big Ed and The Dog lunged forward.

A moment later, Big Ed somehow had Little Dootchy by the heels. He stood, great Hercules with his Antaeus, and swung his enemy round and round his head. As he swung, his fury grew. Faster and faster the face of Raoul Duchesne circled the air. Chris laughed aloud, and the three fascinated women at the door held their sides for the gleeful horror of it.

With a mighty heave, Big Ed let go.

The crumpled figure of Raoul Duchesne came to rest against the butt of the ledge down by the Brook.

The Dog made to leap in pursuit, and fell in his own blood. The shot had been meant for him. It had missed the heart, but a leg bone was shattered. Big Ed picked him up and carried him home.

The Brook lipped at the granite. It lipped a tiny lichen from its place. It supped the unfamiliar taste of waxed hair. It felt the heft of the lolling head, and bathed the blood from the tooth marks on the throat. It spewed out the bubbles of air that came up through the broken neck. It ran under the bridge.

The three in the chamber at the front of the house knew not of these happenings. Mary had passed the doctor's words on to the kitchen, and closed the door. She and Doc had heard the shot, but they had no time to wonder what it meant.

Mary sat at the bedside, her hand on Judith's pulse, her head bowed in supplication. Doc Sanborn clutched the footboard with clenched hands, his knuckles mottled with purple. There was nothing more that he could do. There wasn't any next thing now. This life had been taken out of his hands when the last blood trickled. All, now, was up to Him.

The first fingerlings of sun picked out the lovely colors of the Persian rug. They lit with tiny points of silver the lashes that lay against the motionless cheekbones. The pulse under Mary's finger fluttered and was still.

Judith Duchesne watched the pointed flame of a candle, burning bright. She was sitting in the wing-backed chair in Mary Jewell's sitting room, and a voice was reading to her from a book. No. It was singing. "He fill yer mother's titties up with milk. . . . He put the lovin' heart inside o' you. . . . Breathe easy now. . . . Breathe easy. . . . ''

The voice died down to a whisper she could not hear. There was still the candle, in the heart of its quivering flame, a bright red spot.

The candle itself went far into the distance. Only the red spot could be seen. Tinier now, and tinier, farther and farther away. Till a vast loneliness crept like a beast before its tiny light, and it went out.

Terror upon terror upon terror washed with the sounding of great seas. Judith Duchesne fought back.

The pinprick of the candlelight returned. It came on toward her, so slow, so slow. As it came, it brightened up to red, then to quivering flame. The spot that was so much like blood faded into the steadying flame. The candlelight came clear.

"Ellery," Mary cried, "It's coming back. Feel it . . . feel it. It's coming back.''

Doc Sanborn's fingers were less steady than the pulse and in a shaken voice, no more than half conscious of his words, "Breathe easy, child," he said.

The eyelids of the morning opened wide.

Twenty-eight

THERE never was a court of justice in any land more square than when three New Hampshiremen passed judgment on their peers. It was a solemn convocation in the old Town Hall the day William Jewell, head selectman of the village, Clessie Peters, and George Goodwin, from up in Burnhap District, got together to make inquiry into the death of one Raoul Duchesne.

William Jewell spoke first. "Gentlemen," he said, "by rights I have no business to pass an opinion on this matter. I'm downright prejudiced, I am. So's Clesson, here, I figure. Well, George, Clessie an' I, we've decided to ask for your opinion first."

George Goodwin was the town's Good Man. A saint, they said of him, with human ways, a man of charity. "Well, boys," he said, "I took it on myself to ask Doc Sanborn to come here this mornin'. Reckon he'll be back from Schoodac any minute now. But I can say, right off, that I misdoubt it's any occasion to call in the law from outside. No reason why the matter can't be kept inside these here walls. Has Mrs. Duchesne expressed any wishes?"

Doc Sanborn stood in the doorway. "I didn't deem it wise to acquaint my patient with the whole story." he said. "She's pretty low. Still livin' somewhere she can't be reached, an' I don't aim to disturb her on a subject that will tax her strength so fer. Mrs. Jewell and me, we've told her that he died by accident. When it happened, she was clean out of her head, and didn't hear the shot he fired. I brought the only witness who saw it all: your boy, William. He's downstairs now, if you'll consent to listen to what he has to say."

Chris told the story as he'd seen it.

"Think careful, son," George Goodwin said when Chris finished.

"Think very careful. Can you say for sure that that shot was fired *before* Big Ed got hold of Lit...of Mr. Duchesne?"

"Oh, yes, sir. Yessir."

"Well, that's all you need to say, boy. Now, Doc, what about the medical examination?"

"One thing I can say right now, gentlemen," Doc said. "I'd lie in my belly about this if I had to. But happens I don't have to. I give it as my honest opinion that The Dog busted his neck the minute he got a hold on him, like he did that bulldog. An' anyways, even if he didn't, even if his neck wasn't broke when he hit the rock, them toothmarks went too near the jugular vein to be comfortable. An' one thing more I'm goin' to say, an' to hell with the law, if it be so that the boy kilt him with that heave, that were an act o' God, an' not intentional on the lad's part."

"Waal, then, "George Goodwin said after a moment, "since you ask my opinion about this thing, I'd say that justice has been done, with mercy thrown in."

Years later, Chris found this entry in his father's diary:

SEPTEMBER 12, 1883.

Had a meeting of Selectmen today to settle the matter of Raoul Duchesne, who died last night in Schoodac District. It was deemed he met his end by unavoidible accident. We adjourned without further business.

The writ had run.

Twenty-nine

CHRIS flailed beans on the barn floor with an energy that smacked of desperation. He couldn't think of any other place to look for Big Ed. Just when he had got his chores out of the way on the morning of Little Dootchy's death, and had been going to ask his father's permission to follow the trail of blood that led from the grave of the fawn in the direction of Kearsarge, Doc Sanborn had come to ask him to testify at the selectmen's meeting. By the time he had got back to the trail, it was faint on the dry pasture ground, and it stopped altogether at the Brook, up under Iddo's pond. Iddo said he'd seen them when he went to let his chickens out, just disappearing over the mountain. Ed had been carrying The Dog.

Ten days had passed, and Big Ed hadn't come home at all.

"I'm bound to say I'm worried about the boy," Ed's father said. "He ain't bin like hisself lately, atall. On'y time I ever had to fret much was the times he got to talkin' to hisself. I never thought much when he didn't eat. Never did eat what you'd call proper for such a great body. But sence that deer died, he ain't et a morsel, to my knowledge. I could see he was all ga'nt up, but I callated he'd git over that. But talk! Why, he kept talkin' alla time, by God. Seems he was talkin' to *somebody*, but I couldn't make it out. Talked about God a lot, like his Aunt Fanny learned him to."

"My mother says she thinks he'll come back when the moon's high enough. But she's kind o' worried, I can tell."

Mr. Cheney rapped the bowl of his pipe on the porch railing. "We could hitch up Betsy, one o' these mornin's, and go lookin'. That's if yore pa says you kin."

William Jewell said yes, Chris could go. So they went, making a full circle, around the base of Kearsarge over to Salisbury and Bradford and Sawyer's Mills and Joppa and Henniker and Hopkinton; and back through Weare and Weare Center and North Weare.

"A great big boy an' a dog," a woman over Joppa way had said, "why, yes. Though I don't guess I'd o' taken him fer a boy. More like a man growed old afore his time. Stooped like. His hair all fallin' round his face. Kinder pitiful, he wuz. An' the dog, goin' on three legs. Fierce? Goodness, no. Laid down and whined. 'Twas close to suppertime an' I asted 'em in, but they wouldn't stop. Wanted the feller to have a bite ter eat, with my man an' me. But all he'd take was a slice o' bread with some jelly on it. Couldn't talk right. All he said wuz, 'Please, ma'am, you dot a little bone fer my dod?' Funny, the way he thought fust of that crittur."

No one else they talked to around the rest of the circle had seen anything of the pair. Mr. Cheney speculated that they might have gone upstate somewhere, but it was more likely, he thought, they were just hiding out in the woods, and would reappear in a day or two.

That hadn't happened.

Thus the extra spurts of energy that went into the flailing of the beans. Not that Chris's world lacked targets for his energy, harvest being in full swing. The fruit seemed to ripen all at once. The apples came in a steady run: Red Astrakhans, then Gravensteins and Northern Spies, russets and blue pearmains, and, finally, the heavy crop of Baldwins. Windfalls had to be gathered and carried to the cider mill. The field corn across the road from the Duchesne house remained to be picked and shocked. His mother asked him, whenever he ventured into the kitchen, for more food for the kettles seething on the stove. Chris didn't have an idle minute.

Aching with weariness, he would tumble into bed at night and wait for sleep, always listening for the sound of singing. The September moon grew from earthshine to pallid glow to shimmering radiance, and still there was no sign of Big Ed.

Thirty

THE same light that had fallen
from April's eyes on the yellow buds of the biggest elm tree in New
Hampshire now fell in late September on its yellow leaves. Mellow and
fine, like spun threads of the sugar that was golding up the world, it was
acquainted light, having known summer's multiform birth-days, and all
the inenarrable glad run and rut of fruiting earth. When it reflected from
the great umbrella of the tree through Judith Duchesne's front windows,
it caressed the mahogany headboard, and muted down the weft of rugs,
and seemed to speak of ultimate things as it wandered over counterpane,
silver-mounted toiletries, and the moss rosebuds on the commode set. It
rested tenderly, with all its burden of old sympathies, on the dark hair,
touching also the tip of the fine aquiline nose, and brushing the
cheekbones with its patina.

But it brought no color into that face, no heightening of blood.
Judith lay supine in her handwoven linen sheets, scarcely moving for long
hours at a time one finger of the hands that rested at her side.

Doc Sanborn came daily to look at his patient, and Mary Jewell,
leaving her menfolks to Phronie's care, was almost always at the bedside.

"Mary, I been thinkin' a lot about this case," Doc said one
morning. "I never had one quite like it in all my days. I've had folks that
wanted to die, but allus for a reason I could see. You remember Belle
Howe, who pined away after her boy was killed in that train wreck. She
just up and died. And a good thing, too: she'd had a life of misery and
had nothin' to look forward to. But Judith. What's ailin Judith?"

"I've got my theories, Ellery," Mary replied. "Sometimes I think it
was too bad we had to tell her how her husband met his end, even if we
did fancy it up a mite. Women are a funny lot, as you know better'n
most men. I think she got so used to taking up gussets in herself, so she

could bear to live with him, that the night they came home from the fight, she took up one too many. Like as not, she had got used to her husband, and set her ways by him. She told me that morning that she hadn't any more 'ghosts', whatever she meant by that. I guess she outdid herself that night. I think, Ellery, there ain't a woman ever lived, no matter how meanly her marriage turned out, but had a feeling afterwards that there was something she could have done, something that would have made it better."

Doc Sanborn mulled that over. "I suppose you're right, Mary. Yes, I suppose you are. You ever hear of a body dyin' of too much peace?"

"No," said Mary. "But I've known plenty of women that have fainted dead away when they unlaced their corsets."

Doc smiled. "Waal, something like that," he conceded. "Just between you and me, Mary, I'm not the least sure we can do anything to keep her here. Excuse me for sayin' this, Mary, but you're lookin' a mite peaked yourself. I did somethin' this mornin' you may not like. I spoke to Sarilla and asked her if she could come up here and help out for a spell. That ol' fat satchel ass—pardon me, Mary—she's a damned good nurse, almost as good as you. Of course, we haven't any idea whether that man left her any money or not; but I'll be glad to take on the expense, for a few days at least, while you get some rest."

"I'd thought of that, too," Mary assured him. "We'll all share in paying her, though you know as well as I, when Sarilla likes a body, she won't take pay, except her keep. I've still got pickles to put up, and all those green tomatoes to make into piccalilli, and the apples are just right for apple butter. Phronie can't do it all, though Phronie's good as gold. Besides, she's got her own to do. Mr. Jewell says she doesn't talk a mile a minute anymore, only about three-quarters of a mile. I've got another idea about Judith I haven't tried yet, but I'm not going to tell anyone till I've tried it, not even you. I won't give up. You can count on that."

"It won't be us as'll have anything to do about it," Doc said wearily. He rose to go. "Jest give her all the nourishment she'll take, Mary. Watch that pulse. Keep your niter handy. Try to get her to take some of that port, for her blood. Anything else you think of will be all right. There are times, Mary, when I think of women, like you and her, and my little Amity, I wish to God I'd been born with teats. 'Twould have made a man of me."

Mary went with him as far as the porch, then went back and sat down by the bed. She took one of Judith's hands in her own and began talking softly but gaily of the things that were going on around the farm. She told about the apples, how good they were this year, and how the cows had got into the orchard and stuffed themselves with windfalls and got as drunk as lords and all their milk had had to be thrown out. She told how good Phronie was, and that the fine nourishing soup that Judith had was a secret receipt Phronie had never given to anybody. Some sort of hex she put on it from her herb bed, Mary suggested.

Judith smiled. "I want to see Bid Ed, Mary, if he will come," she said.

Mary tried to give her reply a casual sound. "Oh, he's off wanderin' somewhere, the way he does, you know. He's mostly gone at the dark of the moon. We heard"—and this was the truth—"he was over near Ami Brook the other day, over Henniker way, you know. Mr. Jewell's cousin said he showed up at her door, and asked her if she had a bone for The Dog."

"The Dog was . . . was hurt, wasn't he, Mary?"

Mary devoted a swift thought to tongues that couldn't keep themselves at home in folks's mouths. "Yes," she said, "but he gets about nicely on three legs. We had an old collie once, got run over by a dump wagon. Lived for years, happy as a lark. Could outrun and outhunt any dog around." She paused a moment, and changed the subject. "Well, well, it just doesn't seem possible winter's so near. Goodness, it won't be long now before we'll all be cozy as bugs, quilting and catching up with the mending, and all. I reckon my brother will be home before long. We'll be having our readings again, Sunday nights. The popcorn's never been so fat on the cob."

There, she'd said it. As casually as she could manage, and it had brought a smile, but a smile little different from Judith's usual sweetness, if any. Mary tried to imagine the news brought a little color to Judith's cheeks, but she had to admit that it was rather the way the wind outside had tossed the branches of the elm, letting in a dappled whisk of light.

"My brother often speaks of you in his letters," she persisted. Judith made no sign, so Mary took up her whole courage, and said, "In fact, if I read rightly between the lines, he thinks about you more than's good for him. I'm bound to tell you, young lady, that distance seems to have lent a good deal of enchantment to his thinking about you. I know he's itching to come home, but he just wanders from place to place, Vienna, Geneva, Paris, and I have my notions why. Well, I'm going to leave you to take a good sleep. If I don't watch out, Phronie'll be making another hasty pudding for my men, and Mr. Jewell says the very sight of her, stivvering out to the barn after corn meal, is enough to set his teeth on edge."

She left, wondering whether John had received her cable. It seemed impossible to her that he could have, so great was the distance, but, small though her faith in mechanical marvels might be, her heart told her in no uncertain terms that John, at that very moment, was on the high seas, forging westward.

Sarilla moved her vast breasts and buttocks, bag and baggage ("rags and raggage," Bart said), into the Duchesne house the next morning. Mary went over to give her such instructions as necessary, though Doc Sanborn himself had brought her up from The Corners, and there wasn't much to tell her. Doc stayed only long enough to unload Sarilla's belongings, but Mary sat down and had a cup of tea with her.

"I can't imagine anything will do her more good than that laugh of yours, Sarilla," Mary told her. "I guess we've all had too much on our minds to do much laughing these days."

"Funny thing, Miz Mary," Sarilla said, pulling at a hair on her lower chin. "You know, when they first came here, Mr. Duchesne asked me to come up here three days a week. Waal, when I was ready to leave after the second day, he come in and said his wife had changed her mind, she didn't want me to come no more. *He* said it. She didn't say a word.

I'll do onything I can . . . onything."

"Yes, that's the way with all of us. And there's one thing you can do for her, sometime today, if she seems wide awake and just thinking. Here's a pack of letters, from a friend of . . . well, of hers and mine. Just put them on the table by the bed, and tell her I thought she might like to look through them. Don't say any more. Just leave them there. But I tell you something, Sarilla: you keep the door open just wide enough to see through a crack, and you keep an eye on her while she reads them, and let me know how she acts."

Sarilla was an eager accomplice. Mary headed home, her hands dancing under her apron. She had a smile on her face like a naughty child.

Thirty-one

IT was almost four o'clock the next afternoon before Mary got away from her own kitchen and was able to go over to get a report from Sarilla.

"Far's I know, she didn't read but one o' them, an' only half o' that," Sarilla said. "Fust off, 'twar like she was took by surprise. She read a bit, an' then she kind o' lay back. I thought she'd swooned herself, I did. I hurried in an' gave her a dose o' niter an' rubbed her hands, 'twere ice-cold they were. Waal, she come to aright. But, mercy on me, Mary, I was half a mind to take 'em away. 'Twar close to dinner time, an' I brisked 'round an' brought her some soup. I mus' say, she et it all up 's if she liked it. She's bin asleepin' all the arternoon. I'd say she were a bit steadier'n this morning mebbe. I reckon them letters, whatever they be, was pretty strong medicine."

"Did she say anything?" Mary asked.

Sarilla reflected a moment. "No, she didn't say nothin' 'bout the letters," she said. "She did ask me who made the soup, though."

Mary went in and sat beside the bed, unenlightened. She allowed herself for a moment to doubt that John had received her tidings and was on his way home. But she rejected that possibility out of hand—it was too devastating—and turned her attention to her patient.

It was hard to tell about a woman who hadn't any natural New Hampshire red in her face, even at its healthiest. Did she only imagine a delicate blow of color on Judith's cheeks? She had. The big east-looking room was dim in the afternoon light, the day having been a sullen one, with breasts of heavy clouds bulging with rain. Mary wanted to try the pulse, that told so much, but Judith was sleeping like a tired child, and Mary believed she wasn't, couldn't be, mistaken about the look of . . . well, of life, and rest, on her face. Ellery had wondered if folks died of too much peace. Well, it wasn't exactly peace that fiddled like a faint tune on Judith's brow. Mary was glad she had brought the letters. If they'd done nothing else, they'd taken her mind off other things.

The hand on the counterpane turned over. Suddenly, almost convulsively. Mary held her breath and reached for her bottle of spirits.

Judith was smiling awake. "Hello, Mary," she said.

Mary put the bottle down. "My, you've had a good sleep, haven't you, Judith? That's the way. That's what the doctor ordered. Sarilla," she called.

But Sarilla was already in the room, bearing two tall goblets of grape juice. Having served them, she went back to the kitchen.

"The Concords this year," Mary said, "they've never been better. That vine was planted by William's great-grandfather, a good hundred years ago."

Judith let some silence go by to show that she already knew the history of the grapevine. Then she said, "I feel like talking, Mary."

"You just go right ahead and talk, just so you don't tire yourself," Mary counseled.

"About . . . about my husband."

"If you want to. You don't need to, you know. Later, perhaps."

"No. Now. I...I wasn't.a...a good wife for Raoul."

"Gracious me, child, there isn't such a thing as a good wife. Nor a good husband, either, for that matter. But go on."

"Well, when I married, I was...well, completely ignorant. I...I hadn't the remotest idea of...of what marrying really meant. And when I knew..."

"When you found out, child, you were so ashamed you couldn't bear it. Isn't that it?"

"Yes. Yes. I tried, Mary. I did try. Such a mess I made. It seems the more I tried...the worse..."

Mary laughed outright. "Now you stop vexing yourself, child," she said, "and listen to an old married woman for a spell. I never thought to say this to anyone, and, God willing, I'll never have to again. But I've been married to Mr. Jewell now some nineteen years, and I can't bear it yet. At least, I'm just getting where I can. I'm not in love with my husband, not the way the storybooks go on about love. I was just luckier than you. My husband is a good man, in every way. When I first met him, I had been too...well, too sheltered, the way girls are. I came up here to visit a girl I'd been to school with and met Mr. Jewell. He was tall and strong and good-looking, in his country way. I hated my father, and I was ready to take any man who would get me away, clean away, from home. Why, Judith, I've spent nineteen years trying to make up to him for...for the way I feel about...well, about what you're speaking of. And we aren't the only ones, either. I don't know as I care, this minute, if I do say things about the...the dead that aren't exactly complimentary. I've never had to be jealous myself, or cause jealousy. But my father was jealous of my mother, not as bad as Mr. Duchesne, but bad enough. And I have known ever since I was a child almost, that if the Bible ever said a true word, it was about jealousy. 'Cruel as the grave.' "

Judith sighed and folded her hands. "You knew?"

"I knew. Now you listen carefully to me. *You did the best you could. I know, now, what happened that night.* He beat you on the head, so no one would see. I didn't even tell the doctor what I found when he told me to cut out some of your hair. And you thought you had to take it from him, because you didn't like to go to bed with him. I can see you now. You just stood there, and grew taller and taller in your mind, trying to get so's you could endure . . . always and everything. He couldn't stand it to see you like that. He tried to break you, and you wouldn't break. But you almost did, my dear. You lost all sense. You tried, like all us women they call strong, to be God. Maybe you won't believe it, seeing me now, but when my children were taken away, I tried so hard to see the thing as God saw it, that I ended up by going off my head entirely. You ask Doc Sanborn. They caught me, the middle of one winter night, in my nightdress, going round and asking the neighbors if they'd seen God around anywhere.''

"Why, Mary. No!"

"Yes. But death itself is not the worst thing, Judith. There's much in life that's worse than death. They call me a good woman, a strong one. But I couldn't have stood what you've been standing. I just couldn't have, and I know it."

Mary stole a good look at her friend. She had more to say, but it could wait. "There now," she said, "I don't want to tire you out."

"But I'm not tired at all," Judith claimed. "Tell me . . . tell me the rest."

"Oh, there isn't much left to tell. Go on, have your remorse, if you must. Everyone does, every single human being does. Why, Judith, when I would begin to think of how I'd spanked my little boy—not Christopher . . . of all the cookies I didn't let the children eat, just because I wasn't hungry . . . of little things they'd wanted to do and I too busy with the housework . . . why, every time those things came into my mind, I died, myself. But I guess, Judith, it's only by dying in life that we grow up. We aren't born saints, you know. Why, Judith, you're still in your twenties. It's no use trying to tell you now how all this will seem to you, say, ten years from now. But you're way far ahead of most women. Have you any idea, child, of how you're loved in this community? Come with us, my little sister. With funny waggle-tongued Phronie, and Sarah, who needs you . . . and now you practically have to traipse along with me, to keep my secret for me. Why, we've got so much to talk about, we won't catch up in forty years."

She bent and kissed the quiet cheek. "I guess that's about enough for once."

But Judith didn't let her go. "Mary," she began, "those letters..."

"Yes?"

"I couldn't...I couldn't...do it again. Marry, I mean."

"Of course you couldn't, child. Of *course* not." The wisp of what might have been a smile came and went on Mary's face.

"There'll be enough...money..."

"Mercy, that's good to know. You haven't any idea how good we'll all feel about that. Phronie and I were terribly afraid you were going to be one of those women that spend their lives taking care of old aunts and destitute cousins and drooling old men. You sure you haven't got any such that'll come running the minute word gets about that you've got a spare chamber?"

"I'm all alone, Mary."

"You're no such thing. And I might say, as knows, that you don't know my brother John. He's had his own bad time. And I can see him, at the age of ninety, hobbling around with a cane, adoring you, and never asking a thing of you, unless it be he'd like to read a poem to you now and then. There, that's enough of that. I've got a breast of chicken left over from dinner, and some applesauce I made just this morning. Sound good?"

"Good enough to try, Mary. Just now, I feel wonderful."

"A woman never feels quite so good as she does the few days after her baby comes."

The door opened a cautious crack, and then wide. Doc Sanborn came in. "What's this?" he said by way of greeting. "What's goin' on here? Tryin' to put me outer a job, Mary? Does it every time, Judith. Let's feel that pulse." He did so. "Hmmm...all right. Best calm down a mite. Sarilla...hey, you fat ol' fool, Sarilla...bring Mrs. Duchesne a glass o' cool milk, not cold, an' put six drops o' that stuff in the little green bottle into it."

"We missed you today, Ellery. Who's been having a baby all day?"

"Percy Higgins's wife." The doctor was now seated, still holding Judith's wrist gently in one hand, still counting. "Twinnin' again. That makes her thirteenth, if I count right. Thirteen snotty-nosed redheads, half on 'em no brighter'n they might be. Younguns all over the place, peepin' in the window while she dropped them boys. They do say as 'man proposes an' God disposes', an' there come a time, round noon today, when I could o' wished Percy had never got beyond the proposin' stage."

"And my one . . ." Judith ventured.

"Godamighty, young lady, I'll be around to spank your tenth, you wait an' see," Doc admonished. "Why, that fool Higgins woman lost two 'fore she borned one alive, an' had her first set o' twins on her thirtieth birthday. Little mite of a thing, too, about ninety pounds soakin' wet. Thanks, Sarilla. Now fetch yourself and Mary here a glass o' port, to celebrate . . . an' bring me that bottle o' rum under the pantry shelf. Your doctor, young lady, is goin' to get looplegged drunk tonight, as Bart would say."

Mary walked with him to his buggy. "You think she's on the mend now, for sure?" she asked, expressing her hope.

"I'm comin' over and have supper with you folks, Mary. She's too high up for my likin'."

"Oh, dear, I guess I talked too much."

"You never talked too much in your life, Mary. I calculate she had to talk. No, she's still way down under somewhere. She'll have a relapse any minute now. Run in an' tell Sarilla to fetch me soon's her pulse goes down."

By the time Sarilla came waddling over to fetch him, Doc had drunk down half a pitcher of the Jewell's best hard cider, and Bart, to be sociable, had drunk the other half. Doc Sanborn was nonetheless able, by means which he himself could not have described, to rally his patient and bring her back to shore, at least temporarily. In her delirium, she had asked over and over again for Big Ed.

"Don't *anyone* know where that fool boy's gone to?" Doc asked when he was back in the Jewell kitchen. "She's got him on her mind, an' he got some sort o' spell he casts. Goddamn it, someone go an' fetch him back. This can't go on much longer."

Thirty-two

"GODDAMN that pesky bird," Doc Sanborn said, his eyes apparently trying to focus on the bridge of his nose. He was quite drunk again. "If I hate anything more'n sin itself, it's a bird hoverin'. Flappin' his wings an' just standin' on the air, an' screechin'. It's unnatural, it is."

"You *would* think he'd go home to bed," Mary agreed. "But the moon's bright enough tonight to fool even the . . . the hawks. Just hear the roosters crowing. Silly things."

"That ain't no hawk, an' you know it, Mary."

"Yes, I know. But this isn't any time for superstition, either," she said sharply. "Just because a bi . . . a buzzard smells a dead rat." She'd almost said bizzard, as Sabina Dow would, and she shivered.

"Buzzards don't smell. They *see*."

"Well, that's a relief, if it's true, Ellery. It's certain he can't see into this ·house. I've got the shades all drawn."

Phronie, rocking back and forth in the kitchen chair, decided to pour herself some tea. When she got up, the chair kept on rocking. Sarah Peavy jumped up and put a stop to it. "I jest can't stand a chair rockin, when there's no one bottomin' it. What's more, it's a bad sign," she said.

The silence was a palpable gloom. October had come and the night was unwontedly cold. The cornstalks, cackling their sear deadsong on the uplands, swayed in strophe and antistrophe with the whistling wind.

"I'm beat," Doc Sanborn confessed to the company. "An' I ain't never been clean beat before. No sir, I ain't. Somepin hellish, it is. By God, she's healthier'n any one on us here. I swear she's put on weight. God rot that man! He must o' kep' her in that sinkhole mind he had until she can't get out. An' what in tarnation hell Big Ed's got to do with it, that beats me, too. She's callin' for him again tonight. She's wild tonight, plumb wild."

Sarilla came to the door. "She's asking fer you, Mary."

Judith was sitting up straight in bed, her hair falling in its black cascade around her, running its rills of liquid ebony in the dim light of one candle. She was as calm, as much herself, as Mary had ever seen her. When she spoke, the sweet low voice was once again the voice of Judith Duchesne.

"He's coming, Mary," she said. "He'll be here any minute now. Tell Sarilla she'll find the cocoa on the third shelf, behind the saleratus can. He likes four heaping teaspoons of sugar in each cup. I hope there's a piece of some kind of cake. And a bone. Above all, a bone. Oh, Mary, I didn't kill . . . this one. I didn't kill him."

While Mary searched for a response, she heard from the kitchen Chris's excited cry: "Hey, Big Ed's coming! Him and The Dog!"

It was a right good thing, they all agreed, that Judith couldn't see very well that night, in the light of the one candle. When Ed came into the room, only his great height was plainly visible. But the others had seen him in the brighter light of the kitchen, and were struck dumb with what they saw. A great wraith of a man he was, and not a man at all. His cheeks were sunken, and on them burned the red of unmistakable fever. He tried to close the door behind him, but no strength remained in his great hands, and he staggered with weakness. The Dog, too, hopping along on three legs, was like the ghost of what he had been. There was something in the eyes of both like white fluttering birds, burning and wild and ominous.

They knelt by the bed. Judith acknowledged them with her eyes, then placed one hand on The Dog's head, and lay back on her pillow.

They sang her to sleep. They used no words, but soon the house was pervaded by a humming, as though the fur of honeybees was giving voice to nectar from the hearts of all the flowers that blossomed in loveliness, as though the tiny hairs in a fawn's ears had fiddle throats, as though the warm milk from all the little titties of the earth dropped gently, gently, gently, to give life.

Judith slept, a smile on her face. The singing stopped, abruptly, and Ed fell to the floor. Doc Sanborn rushed to his side, almost falling himself in his hurry. A moment later, he asked for help in moving Ed to a couch. Chris ran for his father and Uncle Bart.

By the time Big Ed had been hoisted onto the couch in the sitting room, Doc Sanborn announced that there was nothing could be done.

The Dog lay by the edge of the couch. Chris found a bone and offered it to him, but he ignored it. Toward morning, he licked his master's hand, which hung limply down. Finding him not there, he bounded through the open door and ran for the woods. Chris could have sworn he was using all four legs.

Thirty-three

JOHN TRUMBULL arrived the following afternoon. His sister was the least surprised to see him, and the happiest. After a brief but enlightening stop at the Jewell house, he went on to his own, promising to be back for supper. Mary then hurried over .

to the Duchesne house to ask Doc Sanborn to come for the meal and the evening. Doc and John had always enjoyed each other's company.

Later, when the evening fire was dying down, Doc set his glass down and slapped his knees with both hands.

"By God, my boy," he said, addressing John, "I've practiced medicine as best as I could for fifty years, come next May. I 'prenticed myself to old Doc Schwartz over in Concord, the best damned hoss doctor in these parts. I hankered to go down to Boston, to Harvard University, but my pa, he didn't believe in eddication. Thought farmin' was the gift o' the Almighty to man. Ma, she did what she could, sneakin' me a dollar or two outer her egg money when she could get away with it. Goin' without, like every blessed mother born, God rest her soul. You can't tell me folks don't die o' hard work an' broken hearts. Waal, there ain't never bin a day in all my years o' slashin' at pustules an' yankin' babies backsides fust an' givin' sugar-coated pills fer the pip when I hain't cussed myself fer an ignorant ol' fool. I tell yer, John Trumbull, I knowed from the beginnin' what a mess o' tomfoolery us medics had ter practice on the human race, not knowin' any better. I used to read a fair amount, but ain't much time fer keepin' up, what with bein' twitched hither an' yon, like an ol' water-logged plank. But I kep' thinkin' o' the days when things were much wuss than they be now, an' it allus seemed to me that some day somethin' big would come, some blindin' light, like Paul o' Tarsus. Why, I remember readin' 'bout a man named Ambroise Paré, in France, back in the fifteen hundreds; he was an army surgeon in the wars that was goin' on then, an' he interduced the ligature instead o' cauterizin', an' stopped the practice o' pourin' boilin' oil on wounds. But even a feller smart as he was cooked up a poultice made o' puppies' blood and mud. I guess he had something there at that. Got on the right track with mud, leastways.

"I used to cuss at God, an' then I took to askin' Him to work along with me, an' that were a mite better, at least fer the good o' my soul. Sometimes I had a mind it worked, and I guess it did. But all this time, I kep' athinkin' mebbe He'd show the light ter me. Many a time I've took a wee new crittur in my hands, not breathin' so's you could notice it, an' dipped it fust in hot water, then in cold, an' brought its breath up into it. Folks got to thinkin' I had a way with me, an' I got pride, John, the wuss thing a man could have. I got satisfied I could do anything a mortal man could do, an' I stopped readin' an' took to this.'' He pointed one slender thumb at the bottle on the table.

"An' now," he went on, rather wistfully, "my job's about over. Seventy years old, I'll be, in a few days. I done what I could, I guess, bein' ignorant. An' I can tell you, John Trumbull, that I got humility these last few years, an' that tonight, when you've told me that some feller smarter'n me, an' young an' all his life afore him, has hit on somethin' that bids fair to go a long way farther than anyone has gone before, I'd like to git down on my knees an' say a prayer o' thanksgiving. Tell me his name again."

"Sigmund Freud."

"Waal, life's a right funny thing, ain't it now! Many a time, Mary here can vouch for it, I've knowed it wasn't anything in a man's body was wrong with him, an' had to give up. You git to thinkin' the way folks around you think—that it's God's will. An' yet you don't, either. You jest know, deep down inside, He couldn't be as ornery as that, not to take a young mother away from her new baby, or let a woman, strong's an ox, pine away."

"Yes, John," Mary contributed. "Ellery's been saying, right along, that it's something deep down in Judith's mind that's been like to kill her."

"By the living Jehoshaphat," Doc cried, slapping his knees again. "To think, here we've been patchin' up the bones o' us poor mortals for's long as history, an' long afore that, an' never stopped to think it were the heart an' spirit is the thing. I knowed it. By God, I did, all along."

I expect you've done a good deal more good than you realize, sir," said John Trumbull. "I wouldn't wonder if Judith would be in a much worse state than she is now, hadn't it been for the understanding you and Mary administered, along with niter and paregoric. You didn't fill her up with poison, the way many of your much more highly educated fellow doctors would surely have done. There is a good deal to be said for the old native witch doctors, you know. They believed in exorcising the bad spirits, and sometimes did pretty well, making a man believe an evil spirit had gone off. Into a herd of swine, for instance. That's just what Jesus Christ did, you remember. And, as I understand it, Judith has got an evil spirit to be plucked out of her. It's a good thing you haven't told her about Big Ed. She might have died of that, believing as she does that she's been the cause of other deaths."

John got up and poured himself a drink out of Doc Sanborn's bottle. Mary spoke: "But what's to be done now, John?"

John walked the length of the oval rug, and back. "I'll have to think it over, Mary," he said. "In a way, it's too bad you showed her those letters. There's a man in Boston who was with me in Vienna, came home with me on the boat. We may have to call him in. Offhand, I'd say I wasn't the one to talk to her. Perhaps you can do it, Doc. Or you, Mary. We don't know much about these things yet. But the first thing is to get her to talk, about herself. One thing I think I can safely say. She isn't going to die. She may have a long spell of coming out of it. It may affect her mind; for a time, anyway. I'll tell you what. Tomorrow morning I'll go in with Mary, and just say hello, and see how she takes it.

"That paralysis, according to your description of the case, Doc, is only fear. It may mend slowly, and it may go away like that." John snapped his fingers. "Don t worry," he went on, "you've both done exactly the right things.

"There's something else, Mary, you seem to have forgotten. Your quotation from the canticles, remember: 'For love is strong as death.' Well, love is the reverse side of jealousy, and even if it does burn with a vehement flame, and sometimes burns the whole soul up, even so, the right kind of love, like yours and Doc's, and Phronie's and Sarah's and . . . and even mine, is the stongest thing in all the world. If she didn't have it in herself, it would be a different matter. But, in spite of everything she's been through, she's unspoiled. And she's intelligent and understanding and greatly courageous. I think she'll see it all very clearly. In fact, I'll practically promise you that in six months she'll be laughing at herself. . . . "Say, look who's asleep." Chris was. John said, "It's time I got to bed, too. I've had a long day. The rest of you can stay up all night if you've a mind to."

Thirty-four

WAAL, I declare, Mary, that makes two on 'em," Phronie said.

"Two of what?"

"Why, two dead ones, like Sabina said. I wonder now . . ."

"Thought you didn't think too much about what Sabina said," Mary said, rather tartly.

"Mary Trumbull Jewell," Phronie rejoined, "you know yerself, ain't no one in the District but has had them words turnin' round in his mind night an' day fer four, five months now. Goodness, when I see Bertie screw up his face with that pain o' his, I jest plain hold onter my breath an' pray, every single time."

Mary, thinking of Judith, changed the subject. "Come to think of it, Phronie, I guess, now Sarilla's doing the nursing, we'd best run up this afternoon and pay a call on Sabina. She seemed all done in that night I saw her, as if she'd blow away if you touched her. We can knock on the door, an' if we hear her meandering around, we'll come right on back."

They found Sabina's front door wide open. Through it they saw Sabina, seated, head bowed, a mouse nibbling at the hunk of bread in her lap. The October wind blew in and gently rocked the chair. She might have been snoozing, but Phronie and Mary were not fooled.

"Mary, that's *three!* That's three on 'em, thank God," Phronie exclaimed.

Mary said nothing, choosing rather to busy herself with the first offices to the dead. She misdoubted that Sabina had included herself in the number.

Thirty-five

NEW HAMPSHIRE sat back on her haunches and took stock of the year. A few odds and ends remained to be tied up before the white beast left his white spoor over the earth, but the fall housecleaning was all but done. The oaks clung to their old copper leaves, and the sumac heads hung sodden and near black on barren branch. Against the cobalt October sky, the clean-limbed maples sported in the first north winds, and around the bole of the big elm tree the last wizzled leaves whispered mournfully of deaths to come. The bullfrog by the Brook dug himself in, and his voice was stilled. The last whippoorwill uttered his solemn go-with-God and was heard no more in the night. High across the bright heavens the geese went by, and the woodchuck curled up around his full belly and settled in for a long sleep.

The earth, and all that was in it, relaxed into Indian summer. Mary Jewell, folding her hands serenely under her apron, counted her winter stores, all complacently at rest in two-quart jars and earthen pickle vats in the cellar that ran the whole underlength of the house. Fourteen hogsheads on their racks, seven by seven in two rows, patiently gave the old old taste of oak to vinegar and hard cider. Chris and Bart took the dump wagon and a hundred grain sacks and went into the woods to collect dead leaves, which they packed around the house for warmth. Now and again the sound of hammering was heard, as one of the men replaced shingles on the house or barn. In the woods, brush was cleared away against logging time.

But these tasks were hardly what a New Hampshireman called work. Sitting in the barn door in the sun, husking corn, the hard muscles loosened up, and there was time for laughter and old jokes. The story about how Big Ed had stopped the dogfight began to grow, and Uncle Bart, spitting his utmost spit, would rock back on his butt, and hold his sides.

"By Christ," he said, "it was too bad we didn't think to cut 'em off an' make a mite o' fries. Now, mountain oysters, they be mighty damned good to eat, put in a hot skillet with a bit o' oil. Though I'll be bound to say, I bet Little Dootchy's would o' been bitterer'n hell."

"Probably too pissin' small to make a good mouthful," Willie Pike remarked. "Must be acomin' time to breed that mare o' yours, Will Jewell."

"Reckon she's got the same idee herself, the way she's thrashing round right now," said Will.

Chris, having been let into the talk of grown men, hung his red face over a red ear of corn, and ran his tongue over his teeth, remembering Big Ed and the way he spat that day. Chris had grown up tremendously in the last month, with the sorrow of Big Ed's death and the knowledge that he would be leaving home in a few days. Uncle John was sending him down into Massachusetts to a boys' school. The prospect was exciting, but at the same time it made all the dear things of home come clear to him. In one breath he wanted to go more than anything in the world, and, in the next, he could hardly bear the thought of not being at home. Couldn't bear to think of not logging in the winter with Ed and the oxen, of not going up to Iddo's pond to fish, of never again hugging close to The Dog and feeling the muscles of his throat when he sang with Ed.

So this is growing up, he thought. He supposed he knew what

Uncle Bart meant by mountain oysters. Men seemed to talk of nothing but women and stallions, after the crops were in. Well, thought Chris, he would have other things to think about, especially when he got to school. For the moment, though, he couldn't keep the restless mare out of his mind.

Phronie came bursting headfirst into the Jewell kitchen, almost stumbling on the sill. "Mary, Mary, where are you?" she called. "Oh, there you be. Whaderyer think! What *do* you think? Bertie... *Bertie*, mind ye, has give me the money for a new dress! Why, Mary Jewell, I'm bound I'll set right down an' cry. It's the fust thing he's give to me I didn't *need* sence he put this weddin' ring on my finger, an' that wuz his ma's. It's fer the party. He says he guesses we ought ter fix ourselves up the best we know, bein' it's the fust time we bin *ast* to her house. My, warn't it nice o' her, to think o' havin' a party fer the boy, the night afore he goes away. But, mercy on me, Mary, seems a mite soon fer her to be up an' givin' a shindig. Seems like we'd better git together an' cook somethin' to take."

Mary sat down, her knees spread a little after the manner of tired women, in their privacy. "There's nothing to worry about, Phronie," she said. "Sarilla would be offended beyond words if we butted in. Sarilla's going to stay there, you know. Trust Judith to see all the good there is in a body. She says Sarilla is the *best* cook. Sarilla is in her glory. Judith has asked her to hook two rugs, big ones. One of the house in summertime, and one in winter. She's offered her a *hundred dollars* apiece. Says they'll be worth a good deal more. She's going to hang them up, one on each side of the fireplace in the parlor. Well, I guess it's true, 'a prophet is without honor...' I guess it takes outsiders to appreciate the folks we've taken for granted all our lives. John says her rugs are works of art. That if she'd ever had a chance, Sarilla might have painted pictures that brought big prices. He says that rug she hooked of her own poor little house with the flowers blooming and the big maple behind will land up in a museum some day. Now, think of that!"

"My! My! Schoodac will be a diff'runt place, with her here,"

Phronie exclaimed. Then, in a different voice, she said, "An', Mary, I know I ought ter keep my big mouth shut, but we've been friends for more years'n I like to count. I've allus *respected* ye, Mary, fer bein' a mite close-mouthed. But folks is beginnin' ter talk...waal, I reckon it's wishin' more'n anything you'd rightly call gossip, 'bout..."

"About Judith? And John? Well, you can tell them for me, Phronie, that I'm wishing, too. But John's not one to let his feelings run away with him. And Judith...she's had a bad time, you know. A much worse time than most folks know. All in good time, Phronie...all in good time. Just between you and me, old friend, just between you and me...oh, Phronie, what a fine thing that would be!"

"Hmmm...hmmm," Phronie murmured, laying an index finger alongside her nose. "Do I smell somethin' burnin'?"

She surreptitiously wiped her eyes with the corner of her apron while Mary took her cake out of the oven.

The hunter's moon rolled heavily downsky, vying with all the lights in the Duchesne house. From attic to cellar, the big house gleamed and glistened. Sarilla had spent half the night before polishing every piece of silver she could lay her hands on. Each separate prism of the chandelier had been burnished to a rainbow, and the brass firedogs were as bright as the flames that rose from one of Big Ed's four-foot logs. Mellow and ivory, the set of antimacassars that Judith's great-grandmother had crocheted lay soft and ready to hand and head. The candlelight turned lovingly here and there, turning mahogany to crimson luster, plucking at a thread of eucharist blue in an old rug, resting in simple pleasure upon the faces of the men and women of Schoodac District.

Mary Jewell, in her corner, with her stiff bombazine spread round her feet, and her mother's ruby brooch at her throat, was thinking what the past year had done to them. The year, and Judith Duchesne. Why, they were all young again, tonight. All purified, she thought. Tomorrow the old life would resume. Folks would still hang themselves from attic or woodshed rafters, and girls would bury their unwanted babes out under some hummock in the swamp. Well, you were born yesterday, and tomorrow you will lie under the checkerberry leaves in Schoodac cemetery, and in between is life.

The party was such an event as Schoodac District had not known before. Sarilla, moving about in her old sloppy shoes, fondling the solid silver coffee urn as if she had just given birth to it, took a last, prideful look at the heaped plates of food. Judith hadn't had to tell her to keep it simple, to be content with the foods folks were used to and liked. There was no caviar tonight, only their customary, if homely, dishes. But the heavy damask cloths, the silver, and the candlelight worked an enchantment for Sarilla, and her deferential heart swelled almost to bursting, for she saw that she had created something good.

Judith had asked no help from Sarilla in dressing, and when she came down the front stairs to greet her guests, Sarilla took one look, sat down hard on her kitchen chair, and bawled. Folks said Judith had courage that night, to dress all in white, and everyone thought more of her for doing so, on top of giving the party at all. Her seemly full skirt fell in simple folds about her thighs, and she had pinned a single flower into her bodice, where it tucked close around her slender waist. The lace at her wrists and throat seemed more delicate tonight than starshine, and the crown of her hair was a dark diadem. She had allowed herself but one ornament other than the flower: as she moved about the room, the diamonds in her ears laughed merrily.

Ah, beautiful! John Trumbull thought, intercepting a smile of hers and calling it his own.

And Judith proceeded to laugh her way throughout the evening. Some there realized they'd never heard her laugh before, and it was like the wimpling sun, and like the low sweet murmur of waters. She joined their rustic games, and gave Chris his first dancing lesson, with Uncle John on the fiddle. She dragged Sarilla by the ear to come and eat with the others. She got the menfolks to guffawing with laughter, over what seemed to be nothing at all, and there was no woman present but gazed at her with ungrudging admiration. Somehow, she made Phronie feel her homemade dress was prettier than words, and when she complimented Prudence Peters, she caused her to blush as she hadn't since she married.

She found a reason to reach down and plant a kiss on the end of little Sarah Peavy's nose, and Sarah would gladly have kissed those white velvet slippers, she felt so good.

The party quieted down, the heartiness buried in repletion. John Trumbull whispered to his nephew, and Chris arose, though falteringly, to the occasion. "I ... I think it would be nice, Mrs. Duchesne," he said, "if you played us a piece on the piano."

"Why, of course," Judith responded. She settled herself on the bench and lifted her skirt from the pedals. "This is your party, so you tell me what you'd like."

"Oh ... I ... I dunno. Jest anything."

"Now, Christopher," Judith said, "I've seen you, lying out there on your rock, listening to me. You must have some favorite piece."

Chris shuffled his feet on the rug. "Well, there was one. You used to play it over and over. It was ... it was Ed's favorite."

"Did it go like this?" She played a few bars.

"Yes'm, that's it. That's the one."

"That will be it, then, I'll play it for you ... and for Big Ed ... and for The Dog."

Of the company assembled, only John Trumbull knew what it was that Judith played that night. Or cared, if the truth be known. No other person there had ever heard of Ludwig van Beethoven. But there is a natural ear for music in a New Hampshireman. It's in his speech that runs in dithyrambs. It's in the music of the earth he loves. It's the melody of the serpent on his rock, and the soft harmony of all the birds in the air. The whine of new milk in the pail, and cattle lowing. There were some, sitting there that night, who saw corn tassels blowing, while others felt raindrops on their thirsty hearts. But all heard in it the canticle of love, the singing of a giant and his dog.

And they all saw those two there, the gracious woman with her crown of dark hair, diamonds in her ear lobes, and white velvet slippers on the pedals. And the man who turned her music for her, and never took his eyes from her face.